MY WICKED PRINCE

MOLLY O'KEEFE

For you, the reader. I hope this book makes you happy.

LETTER TO MY READERS

Thank you so much for picking up My Wicked Prince! I really hope you enjoy it. A version of this story was published as a novella in a Royal romance anthology. That version was called Long Live My King.

If you read that book and are feeling bummed about picking up this book - don't worry - it's COMPLETELY different. After the first scene - it's all new with 50,000 new words.

Happy Reading
   Molly

1

Now
New York City

Brenna

I FOUND my stepbrother in exactly the sort of place I expected to find him.

In the belly of a sweaty, filthy club that smelled of smoke and sex.

"I'm here for Gunnar Falk," I told the man standing at the door. Dressed in black, he wore the casual focus of a bodyguard. His long, narrow stare was an attempt to intimidate me. Question every decision I'd made that led me to this particular door. Perhaps he wanted to make me quake in my heels.

But it would take so much more than this man's eye contact to rattle me.

I'd been, after all, intimidated by kings and queens and council members who didn't much care for me the last three years of my life.

I arched an eyebrow and pulled open the fur collar of my coat to reveal the necklace I wore. At the base of my throat was a medallion with a wolf's head and a sword. The seal of the royal family of Vasgar.

"I'm here on business of the kingdom," I said. "Notify Gunnar or I'll have this place emptied so fast it will make your head spin."

The bodyguard bowed his head, which meant he was one of my countrymen, having recognized that only members of the court wore the seal.

"A moment," he said in our language.

"Of course," I said with polite patience that I was far from feeling. But it was my one great skill. Pretending to be patient. Pretending to be polite. When inside I seethed.

Bodyguard turned to speak into a radio device he had tucked into his sleeve, and I fought the urge to roll my eyes. Gunnar, as usual, taking things a bit too far. I wondered if he made his staff bow to him every morning.

For a man who resented being a prince, he sure did enjoy being treated like a king.

I had spent a long flight from Oslo to New York City trying to get rid of all the memories that still lingered from the few months we'd stopped fighting and became...something else.

But standing at this door, three years since I'd last seen him walking away from the palace, it was obvious some memories lingered. There was the sensation of his hand against my face that I couldn't quite get rid of. The glimmer of his smile in the dark. That dance at our parents' wedding.

Those memories that could not be burned on the pyre of

our past would have to be buried. Because I intended to live a very long time, and I refused to be haunted by memories of my worst mistake. The humiliation after all these years was still...

Fresh.

"He's waiting for you inside," the bodyguard said, his eyes respectfully trained on the floor in front of my black-and-red heels. I tightened my jacket again, cinching the belt around my waist despite the sweat tricking down my spine. My fur and my cashmere and my Jimmy Choos—all of it was armor. Over my too-thick thighs and my soft belly and my stupid, stupid heart. I wore the fur hat common in my country, hiding my hair. Because I wasn't revealing any of myself to him.

And at the moment, about to see him again for the first time in three years...it didn't feel like enough. I wanted real armor. A shield from the great hall of the palace. A sword from my ancestors.

Yes. A sword in modern New York City would serve me well.

"Thank you," I said and walked from the dark, dingy entryway down a short corridor that opened up into a room fit for a Roman orgy. Low couches, red and black walls. Dim lighting. It might have been an orgy, actually. There was that much flesh on display.

Of course, I thought, looking right through the scantily clad women perched on the laps of men sitting on couches spread around the room. *What a cliché.*

What did I expect of the man he'd become? Selling his face and his name, cashing in on his reputation as the Wicked Prince of New York.

This was exactly the kind of place Gunnar would call home.

There was a card game happening in the far corner and I checked the players, but Gunnar wasn't there. The men around the table were of average height and average looks and nothing about Gunnar was average.

"Well, well." A dark voice boomed out and all conversation stopped. "If it isn't my dear stepsister, Brenna." All the skin on my body prickled with a sudden fight-or-flight panic. And truthfully, fight barely won.

I wanted to be here like I wanted to be left out on the glaciers to fend for myself.

But this was my job. For the good of Vasgar. And I always did my job. No matter how painful.

I stepped around a pillar and there he was. My body recognized him in an instant. The long three years of trying to eradicate him from my memory vanished with one look.

Him, my body said. *Always him.*

Luckily my body wasn't deciding shit these days.

Gunnar sat at the far end of the long room on—no fucking joke—a throne. Not nearly as ornate or beautiful as the throne of Vasgar, but still a throne. Or perhaps it was just a regular chair, high backed and dark, and it was simply him that made it seem like a throne. He wore a dark suit that made his pale gray eyes look like they were glowing. A crisp white shirt was undone a few buttons, revealing part of the tattoo across his chest. His dark hair was brushed back from his high forehead.

He looked cruel.

As cruel as the day I met him. His full lips, cheekbones that could cut ice, a tall, lean graceful body. Every part of him was too beautiful to be real, like he'd been created for the darkest feelings.

Envy. Disdain. Rage.

Lust.

Mostly lust.

Even now, I could feel it, trying to get inside my armor. The way I couldn't quite stop myself from seeing him with my old lovesick eyes. The way my skin bloomed with a new unstoppable heat that had nothing to do with the temperature of the room.

He was just so fucking beautiful.

And I had loved him so...stupidly.

He twitched his fingers and a woman approached, handing him a glass full of amber liquid, an orange peel twisting in its depths. He smiled at the woman—she was beautiful, of course; Gunnar only surrounded himself with beauty. I was the anomaly. The lone defect.

She wore a red dress that highlighted her long legs and tiny waist. Tits for days. I wondered if she'd been the woman in all those ads. If it had been one woman. Or maybe it had been every woman in this place. I wondered even as I told myself I didn't care.

He lifted the woman's hand and kissed her palm.

But he watched me the whole time, his gray gaze mocking me. Just to see if his knife had found its mark.

I rolled my eyes.

Which, of course, only made him laugh.

With another flick of his fingers the girl was gone, fading into the background with the rest of the beautiful women he used as window dressing. I truly hoped all of them were getting paid outrageous sums of money.

"Gunnar," I said, crossing the floor toward his throne. Of course, the crowd parted in front of me—I'd learned my own tricks over the last three years. I could radiate a kind of disdain that forced people out of the way like an icebreaker in Brinmark Sound.

He would not find me so weak now. So willing.

Not anymore.

In fact, as I crossed the floor, my heels making highly satisfying staccato sounds on the tiles, the smile dropped from his face. His eyes walked all over me, just as I imagined mine walked all over him. Taking in the changes the years had made.

We were the same, mostly. And we were totally different. All at once.

I was still a six-foot-tall peasant with Viking blood. Too big for this world.

And he was still too beautiful. Too cruel. Too uncaring. A king in boy's clothing.

"Gunnar," I said, not using his title. "How not surprising to find you in the basement of some seedy club."

He gasped with fake outrage. "Seedy? How dare you call The Despot seedy?"

"Four people tried to sell me drugs when I came in."

"Well, you look like you need to loosen up," he said. His fingers twitched again and a man stepped to the edge of his seat. Gunnar lifted his chin and spoke into the man's ear and then the man was gone. Vanished up the stairs, I imagined to take care of the drug dealers in the club.

Oh, Gunnar...I thought. But I quickly stuck my thumb in the dam holding back those old disastrous feelings.

"Can I get you a drink?" he asked.

"Not that swill you put your name on," I said.

"You tried the vodka!"

"Calling it vodka is an offense to potatoes."

For a second he almost smiled; I could see it. The brightening of his eyes. The flash of him. The him I knew. And then it was gone. "Champagne?"

"No, thank you."

"Honestly, Brenna, it would not kill you to remove the stick up your ass for one night—"

"Your father is dead."

He blinked at me, and for one second I saw all those things...all those feelings. Dark and dangerous, like sharks deep under the waters he tried to pretend were so still. So uncaring.

But I knew...or I had at one point. I knew what this man hid. And none of his waters were still. He was a storm at sea, pretending for brief moments of time to be otherwise.

"Dead?"

I nodded.

"Well, then champagne for all of us." Gunnar stood and almost before the words were out of his mouth, corks were popping in a corner of the room. The beautiful woman walked around again with fresh bottles. When the woman in the red dress brought Gunnar a glass, he instead reached for the bottle, lifting it to his mouth and taking four long pulls from it.

Again, I refused to feel anything about this.

Not one thing.

A woman brought me a flute and I took it, thanking her.

"You're welcome," she said, slightly surprised, as if it had been a while since anyone had made eye contact with her.

Gunnar lifted his bottle in the air. He was taller than me by a few inches, and with his arm up like that he looked every single inch of our Viking ancestry. The suit couldn't hide it. The thousand-dollar watch. The throne. The bar. None of it hid who he was.

A king.

With five hundred years of Viking blood in his veins.

"To my father!" he said. "May the asshole burn in hell!"

I saw many of the men and women look at each other

before drinking from their flutes. I did not drink. There was no love in my heart for Frederick, but I would not wish him to hell.

"You always were squeamish," Gunnar said, his lips twisting, and I recognized the pain in him that made him cruel. He took another swig from the bottle and then wiped his mouth with his hand. All his sophistication had always been an act.

"Your father is dead," I said, not rising to his bait. "I'm here to take you home."

He shook his head, his eyes bottomless pools of pain he never wanted anyone to see.

But I saw. It was my curse. I always saw him.

"To King Gunnar of Vasgar." I lifted my champagne flute into the stunned silence. "Long live the king."

2

T HEN
  Four Years Ago
  Vasgar

Gunnar

It was the hottest day in July when I met Brenna Erickson.

And I was in the seventh circle of a two-day hangover.

The very last thing I wanted to do was play nice with my soon-to-be stepsister—a third-year law student at University of Edinburgh. Apparently some kind of humanitarian/world politics phenom.

I was bored already.

The air was barely moving, and even in the cool of the palace's ancient great hall, the heat was oppressive. Every window was open in the hope that some kind of breeze could be coaxed inside.

Apparently, it couldn't.

"Why are we in full-dress uniforms?" I asked, standing next to my father, the king of Vasgar, on the wide steps at the end of the hall. It was just him and me standing there. Like toy soldiers. No council. No press. Just Dad and me. In full dress.

"Because we are the royal family of Vasgar."

"And your bride doesn't know?"

"Don't be ridiculous."

More like he didn't want her to forget he was king. The guy in charge.

Dick move, for sure. Though maybe his new queen would get off on this kind of thing.

A thought I spent zero time contemplating.

"Would it kill us to get air conditioning?" I asked.

The throne was behind us. If we took ten steps back, at least we could sit.

The kingdom of Vasgar consisted of two islands high in the North Sea between Norway and Scotland. As king, my father ruled over twenty-four thousand people, six hundred thousand sheep, and a newly found oil deposit off our Northern shore, that we were too poor to do anything with.

"You know how the people feel about changes to the palace," my father said.

"You're marrying a bartender from the South Island. I think they'll get used to change."

"I have been a widower for twenty-six years." My father looked me up and down with his familiar disdain. The fact that I'd survived my birth and my mother did not hadn't been forgiven by my father. You'd think he'd be happy with an heir. But you'd be wrong. Just like I was, every day of my childhood. "I think my people will allow me some happiness."

"But not central air."

Dad didn't say anything.

"When you meet Brenna, be kind," Dad said, and the word *kind* was so ridiculous coming out of his mouth I laughed.

"This isn't funny, Gunnar."

"Oh, Dad, it is. It's pretty funny."

"Just don't be an ass."

"Why would I be?" I asked.

"Because you don't have a reputation for kindness," Dad said.

It was true. I had a reputation for a lot of things—kindness was not one of them. It was a Falk family trait.

"She's not...royal," Dad said.

"Excellent." Royals, as I had become aware, were terrible bores. And there was nothing worse in this world than a bore.

"I'm serious. Before she went to college she'd never been off South Island. She's exceedingly bookish. Her father was a fisherman."

"Most of your countrymen are fishermen," I said.

"You know what I mean."

Yes, I thought. *I know you're a snob. A king who barely tolerates his people.*

"She's not like us," my father said.

"Perhaps it's you who needs to be kind," I said.

When he turned to face me, I kept my eyes forward. As if I couldn't wait to see my new family.

He hadn't hit me in years, not since I turned sixteen and shot up six inches in what seemed like one week. But I could feel him next to me practically vibrating with the desire to hurt me. To force those words down my throat.

I didn't look at him, but, oh, I smiled.

"I'm the king," Dad finally said, meaning he did what he

wanted. He straightened the neck of the red wool uniform he wore with its chest full of medals. He was sweating right into the fur collar.

Well, I was sweating into mine, too. The fact that my blood was mostly home-brewed akvavit made lovingly by my best friend Alec didn't help. But I was twenty-six years old and in good health. My father, on the other hand, had had a heart attack a month ago and increasingly alarming checkups with the royal physician.

"She will be a princess of Vasgar," he said.

My eyebrows shot up. "You're making a decree?" By marriage the best her title could be was Duchess. But as princess she would have more standing. And power. Not shabby for the daughter of a fisherman and a bartender, but still...

"Her mother asked," he shrugged as if it was all no big deal.

Wow, I thought. Dad was a goner. Whipped. I wasn't sure if I was fascinated or a little repulsed.

"You will be her brother," Dad said. "I expect you to act accordingly."

Interesting. How did one act at the sudden appearance of a twenty-four-year-old stranger you were supposed to call sister? I had no idea.

"I can be kind," I said. And, frankly, planned on it. The palace with all of its secrets and intrigue could be a cold and lonely place. Particularly for a sheltered, bookish law student from the South Island. I wasn't a total monster.

"Not too nice."

"What does that mean?"

"It means," he said, jabbing me in my chest full of slightly fewer medals, "you are not to sleep with her."

"Dad—"

"I'm not kidding. The entire country is laughing at you, thanks to that situation with the English princess and that athlete."

I sighed. "One threesome with a member of the British royal family and a rugby player, and that's all anyone talks about."

"That's not all they talk about," Dad muttered.

That was true. They talked about me a lot. And I gave them plenty to talk about.

Gossip and sheep. That's what my country was known for.

Well, and the threesome with its prince, the princess, and the rugby player. That had made international news thanks to a hotel maid with a camera phone.

Father always said I was an embarrassment, and I did hate to prove him wrong.

"Here they come!" Dad said, smiling an honest-to-god smile for the first time in years. I was long past being jealous over the fact that I—his son—could never make him smile like that. It didn't hurt. Or sting. It just...was. I turned and looked toward the wide-open doors of the palace.

My father's bride-to-be, Annika, walked in first. I'd met her a few months ago, when she'd been flown up to meet me and tour North Island. And to subtly gauge the citizens' reaction to my father dating someone.

The citizens had lost their damn minds with delight.

She was a stunning woman, I could admit to that. She was forty to my father's fifty, and she looked twenty. She had the blond hair and blue eyes of most of the South Islanders. She was six feet tall if she was an inch.

The people loved her because she was their very own Cinderella. And my father was clearly head over heels for her and her perky tits.

And everyone loved a love story.

It would help if she came with several million dollars in a bank account somewhere. Because, truthfully, my country needed money so we could manage that oil deposit more than it needed a love story.

But apparently refilling the Vasgar coffers was going to be my job. Or my bride's job, whenever the council got around to finding me one.

Annika stopped at the door and turned, waving her hand at someone behind her.

And then Brenna walked through the front door of the palace with a book in her hand.

Most people, when they walked into the palace, were pretty awestruck.

It's the job of palaces to be awesome. And I had been trained my entire life to reflect the palace. To be the personification of the palace. To strike awe.

That was the point of me and I'd gotten pretty good at it. Hungover or not.

But Brenna Erickson looked up, glanced around, her eyes wide behind her glasses—and then she licked her finger, turned the page in her book, and went right back to reading.

Stepsis does not give a shit.

She had her mother's height and long blond hair. But the rest of her was strong and thick where her mother was thin. She stood in the doorway with the sunlight running right through her summer dress, revealing the long, long length of her legs. The breeze lifted the tail ends of her blond hair, dashing them across her glasses as if attempting to stop her from reading. As I watched, she bent to the side and scratched a bug bite on her ankle.

She was absolutely the opposite of me in every way.

I laughed. I couldn't help it.

Her eyes, wide and blue behind those glasses, met mine. Her cheeks went pink, the only sign she might be embarrassed, and then she went right back to reading.

"Don't laugh at her," my father snapped under his breath just as Annika snapped that book shut.

I wasn't. I was laughing at us. In our stupid fur-trimmed uniforms. It was fucking July! Brenna was the only reasonable one here.

"She'll need to be dealt with," my father murmured.

"What are you talking about?" I asked. Brenna looked like our kingdom in summer.

"Her hair, her clothing, she'll need to lose a stone or two. The glasses. A book, my god, what does she think this is? A hotel? Look at her."

Yes. I couldn't seem to stop. Even if she wasn't my soon-to-be stepsister, my father didn't need to worry about me sleeping with her. Brenna was far from my type. I liked girls with more polish. And who made eye contact. Who were suitably impressed and awed and easily convinced to drop to their knees.

But she was...different.

"Hello!" Annika, my soon-to-be stepmother, walked across the great hall with her daughter in tow. "My king," she said in the old language, bowing before my father.

"My queen," he replied and then lifted her hand to kiss it. My father's eyes twinkled and I felt a little nauseous. Wasn't sure if it was because of my father's obvious horniness or the hangover. "Let me present my son, Gunnar, Prince of Vasgar."

I bowed as I'd been taught since I was a toddler. "Good to see you again, Annika."

"Let me present my daughter, Brenna," Annika said,

turning toward her daughter, who had opened her book back up. "Brenna," she hissed and yanked the book away like Brenna was a toddler.

"Hey!" Brenna protested. "That was just getting good!"

"You'll excuse my daughter."

"I won't," I said quickly, and realized immediately it was the wrong thing to say. Brenna looked as if she'd been slapped, and her mother looked at Brenna with an *I told you so* glare.

That's not what I meant, I nearly said. I should have said, but my father stepped in quickly.

"We have some details to discuss before tonight's announcement and Saturday's gala," my father said into the awkward silence in the great hall. I wasn't buying that for a minute—he wanted to get Annika alone for a proper reunion. "The two of you get to know each other a little better. Perhaps show Brenna the gardens."

My father and Annika wandered off to do who knew what, leaving me with Brenna. Who looked like she didn't know what to do with her hands now that her book was gone.

"I'm sorry," I said quickly.

"Don't be," she said right back, her eyes crackling. "I don't care what you think of me."

"You're lying," I said. "Everyone cares what I think of them."

She tilted her head and I adjusted my collar. "It must be so strange to be you," she said.

"Wearing fur in July? You'd be surprised."

"People show you all this respect that you've never even come close to earning."

I very nearly laughed. Out of shock. I mean, the nerve of her. The absolute nerve of this peasant nobody. All right.

Fuck her. And fuck showing her around. I had better things to do. Like pass out and sleep for a day.

"The book was a nice touch," I said. If her goal had been to show us in no uncertain terms that she did not give a shit about the royal palace and the men who lived there...well, mission accomplished.

She grinned with one side of her mouth.

Yeah, she was one to watch.

"You want to see the gardens?" I asked.

"Actually," she said, "point me in the direction of the library. I've heard it's really good."

"Follow me," I said, taking the doors on the left side of the room. There was no way I could just point her in the direction of anything. Our palace was a maze, built in the 1600s to stop raiders from finding the royal family and the treasure rooms. "You're from Nikenburg," I said, leading her past the dining room toward the library. "I was there last fall to help with the—"

"You don't have to make small talk," she said.

"I don't?" Small talk was pretty much all I made.

"This whole thing," she said, twirling her finger around, "is Mom's deal. Not mine."

"What's your deal, then? If the royal palace isn't enough," I scoffed. Scoffing had protected me against my father's dislike for a lot of years. And I could feel this girl's dislike from a mile away.

"I'm only here until the end of September and then I'm going back to Edinburgh to finish my law degree."

"And then what?"

"Well, hopefully the UN after that. I'm applying for a job in the finance department in New York. Between my law degree and my finance minor—" She stopped. "You don't actually care about this."

"I don't?"

Her future looked beautiful on her. She glowed with possibility. And I wasn't jealous. It was impossible to be jealous when I got every single thing I ever wanted— including a rugby player and a princess.

But my entire life was tied to this island. And dreams of getting off of it were not for me. I'd gone to university here in the capital and then joined the army as every crown prince had before me.

"Big plans for a girl from Nikenburg." Asshole. I was being an asshole. I was my father's son, after all. And I hated it.

Do better. Try harder.

Be kind.

This girl had me on the ropes and I did not know how to act.

But she took no offense at my words. Or if she did, she certainly didn't show me. She smiled, revealing a gap between her two front teeth. An imperfection that seemed oddly perfect on her.

"That's right," she said. "Big plans for a girl from Nikenburg."

The *asshole* after that sentence, while silent, was loud and clear.

I opened the door to the library and stood aside to let her enter.

"Oh, my gosh," she said, looking around at the two-story room full of shelves and tables and comfortable chairs around a giant fireplace. "It's beautiful."

"It was my mother's favorite room," I said. Even though I never met her, I felt like I knew her a little because of this room. "She completely renovated it when she moved to the palace."

"Are you mad my mother is marrying your dad?" she asked, looking at me. I blinked under the force of her attention.

"Truthfully, I don't really care."

She paled again and I got the sense that I'd hurt her somehow.

"Are you mad? About your mom and my dad?" I asked.

She shrugged. "I've heard the palace can be—"

"Cruel?" I supplied. My father's household had a reputation. And I had a part of that. We all learned from my father.

"I could say the same thing about my mother," she said. "That's probably why they get along."

I was not going to spend one minute on how the world could be cruel to a girl like her. Not one minute.

"Would you like to see—"

"Nope," she said. "The tour ends here." She looked around with a happy sigh. "You can tell our parents you did your job, and you can go back to your regularly scheduled life of threesomes and running up tabs at bars in Kolska."

"Wow." I swallowed the very strange instinct to explain myself. "Seems like you did some homework."

"News of the notorious prince is pretty easy to come by," she said.

"Well, then, I'll leave you to the library," I said and started unbuttoning my jacket, revealing my sweaty neck and collarbones. A little something Brenna seemed to notice with suddenly wide eyes, like I'd stripped naked in front of her.

"Unless," I said, leaning against the door, "you want some company. There are some hidden couches in the back—"

"You're not funny," she said.

"I'm not trying to be."

"You're not my type," she said.

"Tell me what your type is and I can try." Flirting was like breathing. It was unconscious, but it was fun to see her blush. To watch her mouth purse like I was something sour she was pretending not to want a taste of.

"My type is a royal prince who goes to Nikenburg and sees that the economy is dying. The schools are in shambles, the hospital is practically a hundred years old—"

"I saw all of that," I said.

"My type of guy would do something about it."

And then she shut the door to the royal library in my face.

3

THEN

Brenna

ONE WEEK into life in the palace I was having to remind myself daily that I wasn't going to live here. This wasn't my home. These people weren't...my people.

It seemed like every conversation was two conversations at once, the things everyone said and the things they *meant*. I was assigned a person to help me acclimate and to dress me for royal functions, except she hated me. All while smiling at me.

I hadn't seen my mother for longer than an hour in days, which normally wasn't a big deal, but here in this foreign place she was the only familiar thing and I didn't even have her.

And the press...

I shook my head, refusing to let what the press had been saying about me take root. The days after the first picture of me came out were the worst. I would walk into rooms and conversations would stop on a dime. And everyone was looking at me. All the time. And trying not to laugh.

It was fucking middle school all over again.

But, I reminded myself as I felt my heart begin to pound —I wasn't thinking about it. I didn't *care* what the Vasgar press had to say about me. I'd gotten good at this, over the years, not thinking about things that hurt. But my body still reacted and as I walked through the hallways of the palace I could feel my skin get hot. My eyes burn.

Like my mind would not acknowledge the humiliation, but my body was processing it.

Instead, I worked on my application for the United Nations job. Daydreaming about New York City. Imagining a life so far away from this place I could forget these two months ever happened.

All I had to do was survive the endless parties. Because the court of Vasgar apparently loved a party. And tonight was the biggest one yet.

And, yes, I was twenty-four years old and head of my class in law school. And, yes, I could speak three languages fluently. And in all three of them all I wanted to say was *Oh, shit.*

Shit for a lot of reasons.

1. The dinners.

Fish and lamb. Fish and lamb. Constantly and on repeat. What I wouldn't do for a hamburger. Or a salad that didn't have anything pickled in it. Seriously. That's how the salads were made in the royal palace of Vasgar. With pickled things.

. . .

2. Watching my mom and the king make eyes at each other.

It was just so endlessly weird that my mother was marrying the king!

Part of me wondered all the time if it was real. If they really felt that much...heat for each other. And part of me was sure it was fake, though I don't know what the upshot was for the king. My mom didn't have money or connections. She had me. And a smoking habit she was trying to kick. It seemed obvious that the king was super into my mom and Mom was super into being queen. So this was a match made in some kind of heaven.

3. Gunnar.

Because he was officially the worst. Before meeting him, I'd had my suspicions. I mean, the stories about Prince Gunnar made it pretty clear, but meeting him only confirmed it.

The. Worst.

It had been hard to avoid him this last week, which had been my plan since that awful day we met. But we had all these functions we had to do together. There were engagement pictures that had to be taken with all of us. Like we were a happy family. And then a dozen interviews. Being around him made me feel hyperaware. Like I was naked and all the hair had been taken off my body as well as the top ten layers of skin. He hadn't laughed at me again. Or talked to me. He didn't even look at me. Except the photographer wanted a candid shot of the two of us and I'd stood there like a tool, like I didn't understand what the word *candid* meant, and he'd slung his arm over my shoulder like we were bosom buddies in a Hollywood film.

"Smile," he'd said for my ears only. "You're living the fantasy."

"Which fantasy is that?" I asked, smiling with probably too much teeth.

"Your bedroom is just down the hallway from mine," he said, and I'd elbowed him in the stomach.

The photographer snapped a shot in just that minute and the front page of the *Vasgar Times* had been a picture of what looked like the two of us teasing each other. He was laughing, with his hands on his stomach like I'd actually hurt him. And I was frowning but my eyes were all sparkly.

It looked like we were having fun. Like we liked each other.

They had no idea, of course, that as a rule I did not have fun. And if I was going to have fun it would not be with Gunnar Falk.

But the papers were forming their own opinion of me.

An opinion I was *not* thinking about.

I stopped in the middle of an endless hallway and looked around. Hoping to find some kind of landmark that might tell me if I was even in the right place. But there weren't any.

"Arrrrgh!" I yelled. And it echoed up and down the stone hallway.

I was lost. Again. Walking from the throne room to my room, it honestly seemed like the hallways all changed. Like it was a different route every time.

"Lost?"

Gunnar.

I took a second to inhale and exhale, to pull myself

together so that not all my weak bits were showing. I even managed to smile when I turned.

In the cold stone hallway Gunnar was shirtless. No shirt. Only loose gray sweatpants hanging low on lean hips. He had earbuds looped around his neck and a towel in one hand. And I tried to focus on that towel so I wouldn't get caught up in the planes of his chest. His abs, with the kinds of ridges and cuts that I thought could only be achieved with Photoshop.

Gunnar had been working out. Or something. Something that made him sweaty. He was very pale, but most Vasgarians were. And he wasn't very hairy. At all. His chest and his arms were smooth. He looked like an alabaster statue. Muscled and slick with sweat.

The joke was, part of me wanted to say *Gross* and turn my nose up. But that part was lying. I had to be honest with myself because that was kind of important to me. Growing up the way I had, honesty had been the only way to survive, and the honesty right now was that I was attracted to the vapid and empty but totally hot royal prince.

"My eyes are up here," he said, and I jerked my gaze away from the fascinating bead of sweat charting a dangerous course down his stomach.

Get it together, dummy!

"What? Yes?"

"Are you lost?" He asked it slowly, like I was dim. But he was smiling because he knew I wasn't. And he took a little delight in knowing something I didn't. I was beginning to think that *he* was a little dim.

"Yep," I said, because there was no point in denying it. "Sure am. Care to help a girl out?"

"Not usually, no. But since you're my sister, I can make an exception."

Everyone loved to throw around the word *sister*. But it was a ridiculous word for our relationship. We were complete and total strangers with absolutely no blood connection and zero in common.

I'd made deeper connections with people on the ferry ride between Gastor and Vileada.

"Follow me," he said and turned down the narrow hallway toward a wider one. The stone all looked the same. Thick gray granite from the quarries at the north end of South Island. There weren't any decorations on the walls. No tapestries. No rugs on the floors. No variations in the stone.

"Is there a secret?" I asked, looking at the floor instead of his smooth, sweaty back. "To not getting lost?"

"Sadly, no," he said. "You just have to live here long enough to get the hang of it."

Then I was going to have to get used to being lost. Because I wasn't going to stay here a second more than I had to.

"You excited about the gala tomorrow?" he asked, and I looked at his back, startled that he was making small talk.

"No."

"Really? It should be a good party."

"I'm not really a fan of parties."

"How am I not surprised?" He shot me a look over his shoulder. All sly gray eyes and dark hair flopping down over his forehead. "You can meet other people your age. Maybe find some friends."

"I don't need friends."

"Not everyone is as bad as I am," he said.

Truthfully, of everyone I'd met, he'd been among the best. Which only told a sorry tale about the people in the palace.

We were walking back through the throne room and I realized I'd gone out the doors on the left side of the room, not the right. Left goes to the library. That's why I got confused.

"What are you wearing to the gala?" he asked.

"You can't really want to talk about this."

"I'm very shallow," he said, holding open a thick wooden door for me. "You should know that about me."

I walked past him and caught the scent of his body as I went by. He didn't smell bad...at all.

"This way," he said when I turned the wrong way. I spun on my toe and kept walking behind him.

"So?" he asked.

"So, what?"

"What are you wearing?"

"A dress."

"Sounds beautiful. Will it by chance be that same black bag you wore for the announcement?"

"No. It will be a different black bag."

He turned to face me and I nearly ran into him. "Weren't you assigned someone?" he asked, like he was angry.

"For what?"

"To fucking deal with you," he snapped. "To make sure you don't wear black bags to state functions. To make sure you don't look like a fool."

I looked away, my throat suddenly thick. I could feel my face getting hot.

"I'm sorry," he said.

"No. You're not."

"They're making fun of you," he said.

"Who?" I whispered. But I knew.

"Everyone!" he cried.

"I don't care what the newspapers—"

"It's not just the newspapers. It's all over social media. There are memes—"

"I don't care," I said.

"Bullshit."

"Maybe I'm just not as shallow as you are."

"You don't have to be shallow to have your feelings hurt."

That stopped me a bit. Like he was worried about my feelings?

Wait...was he worried about my feelings?

Prince Gunnar being worried about the reputation of the royal family I would believe—kind of. But my feelings? No way.

"Porky Princess? That doesn't bother you?"

Enough, some internal referee shouted. Enough. There should be a limit. There had to be. I'd been here five days and I felt like I'd been ground down to sand. To nothing.

I shoved past him and started walking.

"I'm sorry," he said.

No, he wasn't. And I didn't really care. I didn't. Rather, tomorrow I wouldn't care. Maybe I cared right now because he was here and I was lost. And...well, it had been a bad few days.

"Stop!" he cried. "Brenna, please. You've gone too far. Your room is down that hallway."

I turned around and walked back to where the hallway split into another hallway, but Gunnar stood in the cross-roads and didn't move. He pointed to the left and I saw a door that might be mine, next to a window cut in the stone.

"I'm going to tie a scarf to the doorknob," I said.

"Not a bad idea."

"Thanks," I said, not looking at him. Not letting my body recognize him in any way. If my brutal honesty forced me to recognize that I was attracted to the evil prince, then my brutal honesty was also very aware that I was much too good for him.

He didn't come close to deserving me.

"Did they give you someone—"

"Yes," I snapped. "They gave me a lovely woman named Bridget—"

"Oh, god," he moaned.

"You're familiar with Bridget?"

"I'm sorry. She's very strict. And proper and...she wouldn't care much for you."

I laughed at him. "Oh, Gunnar, and people call you dumb."

It felt good to be mean to him because Bridget had been mean to me. And he'd been mean to me. And the whole world was mean to me. And it seemed sort of safe to be mean to him, because he didn't care—not one little bit—about what I thought of him. And that was freeing.

"I'm going to send a friend of mine. She's...very cool. Not on the palace payroll."

I shook my head. "No, Gunnar," I sighed. *Very cool* sounded awful. Sounded worse than Bridget. "Please... don't."

"Too late," he said, and I glanced up to see him on his phone. Texting his very cool person.

Tears burned in my eyes and I wished so hard that they wouldn't. I was better than this; I really was. It was just hard to remember that right now.

"And," he said, still looking at his phone. "She's in. She'll be here tomorrow at noon."

"Great," I said, putting as much bite into the words as I could. "Can't wait."

And then I turned—the right way, this time—and went into to my room. Where I blinked back all my tears, booted up my computer to work on my job essay, and did not spend one more minute thinking about Gunnar Falk and this shitty, shallow palace.

THE NEXT DAY a palace page knocked on my door to tell me that I had a guest waiting for me in the library and that I should bring with me all the stuff I was planning on wearing to the gala. Resisting the urge to throw a tantrum, I grabbed the black dress and my shoebox, and with my stomach in my feet and my hope just as low, I followed the page down to the library.

Why the library, I had no idea, but I was thankful. It was the one place I felt a little like myself.

But what was waiting for me in the library was literally a million times more than a guest. It was a clothing shop and a hair and makeup salon. There was a small army of people all smiling at me like the party could finally start.

"Ingrid?" one of them said, and a beautiful woman with a shaved head stepped out from behind one of the privacy screens that had been set up.

"Brenna!" she said and clapped her hands. She ran down the three small steps to come and stand in front of me. She was shorter than me by a foot, with dark skin and tattoos covering her hands. She wore a black jacket and a slinky red dress that were totally fashionable and looked amazing, but on her feet she wore flip-flops with a big yellow flower on the top.

They were so ugly and silly. Which made them kind of beautiful.

"It's nice to meet you," she said casually. She didn't hug me or grab me or bow...the bowing was ridiculous. All week long when someone bowed to me, I bowed back. I couldn't stop it. She just smiled at me like we were old friends.

"I like your shoes," I said, a little startled by the shoes and the fuck-off power that radiated from this woman.

"You and I might be the only ones in the world who do," she said, looking down at them. "They're just cheerful, you know? And frankly, it's fun to wear something ridiculous to the palace. It makes me happy to see everyone work so hard to turn their noses up at me."

With a sudden wrench in my stomach I missed Edda. My cousin and best friend. Since pre-preschool. Since she moved in next door when I was three and we were flatmates in Edinburgh. Oh, god, friends were so nice. It sucked not having any.

"You're here to dress me for the gala?" I asked.

"Yep. But only if that's cool with you. Gunnar said they gave you Bridget." She made a face that made me smile. Ingrid was Bridget's total opposite. And I already felt more comfortable with her than I ever had with Bridget. More comfortable than with anyone I'd met at the palace.

"Anything is better than Bridget."

"Great! Why don't you show me what you've got," she said.

"Well, I hate the dress." It was the dress my mom bought me the night I was home on break and the king took us all out to dinner when he came down to South Island last year. It looked like a dress a sixty-year-old mother of the bride would wear. I was a wall of black ruffles. It was the worst.

"But I love these," I said and took the red shoes out of the box. They were faux fifties pinup heels I'd bought on the high street in Edinburgh, and they gave me an ass and legs for days *and* they were comfortable. Which basically made them miracle shoes.

"Awesome," she said. "They're amazing. Let's build your whole look around those."

At this point I pretty much loved her.

"I also have these. They were my grandmother's on my dad's side." From the toe of the right red shoe I pulled out a velvet bag. I tipped it and the long strand of black pearls filled my palm.

Ingrid literally gasped. Mouth open, she looked at me and then back down at the pearls.

"Are you ready to look awesome?" Ingrid asked, and for the first time in the week I'd been here, I smiled.

I really smiled.

4

T HEN
Gunnar

I'D BEEN AVOIDING the council most of my life. As the prince I had a vote in all government matters and I usually just voted in line with my uncle, who was the head of the council. But the nine members of the council were constantly trying to convince me of something. Lately there'd been a whole lot of conversation about the oil rights in the ocean off the north shore. And I had made avoiding the council at state functions into an art form.

I'd gotten so good at it that most of the council had given up on me.

But not Ann Jorgenson. The throne room was absolutely packed for the party, but she found me.

"Prince Gunnar," she said, catching me at the dais where I kept a flask of Alec's hooch tucked into the cushions of my father's throne.

The sacrilege delighted me.

If anyone noticed no one bothered to stop me. Or remove the flask.

"Councilwoman Jorgenson," I said, making sure I didn't keep the boredom out of my voice.

"Have you thought about the trip to Brinmark Sound after the wedding?" God, she sounded so eager. Relentlessly eager. Like hope was just in endless supply. And if she tried hard enough I would buy some of what she was selling.

She was the only council member I hadn't convinced of my complete and total irredeemable uselessness. What she was holding on to I had no idea.

There was a royal visit planned after the wedding. My father would be on his honeymoon so I was tagged to make the dreary trip up to Brinmark Sound. It was the port town closest to where the oil deposit had been found and Councilwoman Jorgenson thought that if I went there and talked to the people I would start to give a fuck about everything she wanted me to care about.

The woman could not catch a clue.

"I have," I told her, taking a sip from the flask and then slipping it back between the cushions. She could not mask the look of dismay on her face, which of course was the point. "There's a bar there that I particularly enjoy. Kex. Perhaps you've heard of it."

"I don't care about the bar."

"That's too bad. It's really something—"

Ann stepped closer to me, her straight brown hair practically trembling with her emotions. Agitation made me uncomfortable so I stepped back, but she kept coming until my back was against the throne.

Am I...getting bullied by Ann Jorgenson?

"Your uncle is going to sell our oil rights to the highest

bidder and our country will be stripped of all future wealth."

"Ann," I said, trying to placate her. "I think you might be—"

She leaned forward, her face flushed, and I realized she wasn't dismayed or disappointed with me—she was furious. "Your father will die and this will be your country. You can't be the playboy prince forever. Your people need you. Grow up, Gunnar."

Ann turned and walked away, leaving behind the smell of scorched earth. I blinked, feeling something, I didn't at all like.

The old laws would have permitted me to put her on an ice flow for speaking to me that way.

I missed the old laws.

The flask in the throne was half empty and that just wasn't going to do, so I grabbed it and looked around for Alec. Because this twitchy, burny feeling in my chest needed to be drowned out. I scanned the glittering crowd that filled the throne room. The council members, the entire royal family, including my uncle and his children, special guests, dignitaries from neighboring countries. It was an impressive crowd.

The fucking gall of Councilwoman Jorgenson. Who did she think...?

The thought trailed off in my head. That itching, burning feeling in my chest vanished.

Alec was across the hall, his height and shock of red hair and beard made him stand out in just about any crowd, but it was the person standing next to him who caught my attention and emptied my brain.

Brenna.

In a knee-length silver-sequined gown. With bright

red shoes and black pearls looped around her neck. She was curvy and bright and absolute perfection. The dress was off her shoulders, revealing so much of her creamy skin. A subtle hint of some top-shelf décolletage.

She stood there, laughing at something Alec was saying, with her head up and her shoulders back. The defeated girl I managed to finally find the other day, lost in the castle, was completely gone.

The defeated girl the press had been playing with like a cat toy—gone. Gone like she'd never been there.

"So?" It was Ingrid beside me. "Good?"

"She looks lovely," I said.

"Lovely is a bare minimum kind of compliment," Ingrid groused. "You can do better."

She looks like a queen.

More than her own mother—the future queen—could ever look. And it had nothing to do with the dress and everything the way she carried herself. The spitfire who had walked into the palace with a book, thumbing her nose at all of us, had quickly been squashed by the cruelty of the limelight.

Porky Princess. Swear to God I should have burned the whole world down when I saw that.

But the spitfire was back and my relief was...strange. Awkward. Because I cared and truly didn't want to.

But I wasn't going to say any of that.

"I'd fuck her," I said and looked at Ingrid, whom I'd known since boarding school. I couldn't shock her, we were miles past that, but I could still disappoint her. Which, clearly, I was doing.

"Gunnar! Come on! She looks like a princess."

"She does. You outdid yourself."

"She acts like a queen, you know?" Ingrid said. "Smart. Kind. Assessing."

"Is that so?" I pretended not to care or to have noticed, but I doubted my old friend bought it.

Deiter Magnusson, the palace reporter for the *Times*, was talking to my uncle, but I saw the very moment he noticed the glimmering, glittering soon-to-be princess talking to Alec. Deiter had been slinging most of the mud at Brenna and I waited to see what he would do.

Because I had an impulse to take him out back and knock out a few teeth.

But Deiter did a double take and actually stopped my uncle midsentence and pointed Brenna out to him. The expression on his face was properly awed.

Good. He could keep his teeth.

"Tomorrow's papers won't have a bad word to say about her," I said.

"She's a good person," Ingrid said with a sigh. "I hope this palace doesn't eat her up. I hope you don't eat her up."

"Me?" I feigned shock and she rolled her eyes. "She's not staying. Vasgar will only be a part of her origin story when she becomes a superhero. Go enjoy the party. Alec has outdone himself with the—"

Ingrid shook her head. "Nope. Never again with Alec's homebrew. There's only so many times I can wake up in the bottom of a fishing boat with him. A girl has to learn her lesson at some point."

"Good luck with that," I said. Ingrid and Alec had a kind of doomed love affair happening. Entertaining from the sidelines, but both of them seemed a little miserable inside of it. It made me wonder why they couldn't manage to make breaking up stick. Or staying together, for that matter.

Ingrid went off in search of champagne and I found

myself crossing the room toward Alec and my beautiful stepsister.

"Gunnar!" Alec said in that voice of his that had so little volume control. He always boomed. "You didn't tell me your stepsister was funny."

"Are you?" I asked Brenna, lost in the twinkle of her. Her makeup was understated but it made her skin glow and her eyes glitter and her lips... I blinked. "Funny?"

"Very." She held out her hand and Alec put his flask in it.

"Whoa," I said, catching her hand before she took a sip. "What are you doing?" I asked Alec.

Brenna shook me loose. "Calm down, Gunnar. I'm a fisherman's daughter from South Island. I can drink you under the table and still check the traps at dawn."

"This is not some bathtub wine," I told her. "Alec is—" She pushed my hand away and took a sip, waggling her eyebrows at me over the silver flask. "All right. Your funeral."

She gasped and winced and then handed the flask back to Alec. "For courage," she said in the old language.

Alec repeated it and took his own swig, then handed the flask to me, but I declined.

Between Brenna's eyelashes and Ann's chastisement and, I don't know...some weird sense of the world changing right beneath my nose, getting blind drunk didn't seem like a bright idea.

"Jesus," Alec said. "Is that Ingrid?"

"You know Ingrid?" Brenna asked, glowing like a flame. "She's the best."

"She's a witch," Alec said. "A gorgeous, monstrous witch, and what the hell is she doing talking to that musician asshole?"

Alec was gone without another word, stomping across the hall like the berserkers in his bloodline.

"Should we...stop him?" Brenna asked, watching as Alec's gigantic presence scared the violin player away. Ingrid frowned up at him, her eyes shooting daggers, which was pretty much foreplay for the two of them. They'd find the closest fishing boat and fuck each other silly.

"You could try, but he and Ingrid are dedicated to their tragedy."

"Oh," she said, seemingly made sad by that. And for a second there was a leap in my chest, a horrible spike of jealousy. And I was speechless with the unfamiliar horror of it.

Brenna and Alec?

What did I care if she was interested in Alec? I didn't. The answer was I didn't.

She straightened her back and glanced over at me. "You look...nice," she said.

I looked pretty fucking amazing. The black uniform with the black trim was custom and fit like a glove. The sword helped, too.

"Thank you," I said.

"Are you really in the military?" she asked. Blinking up at me through her glasses. "Or is it just for show?"

"I served three years in Crimea," I said. Best and worst three years of my life. It's where I met Alec. Saved his life, actually. But we didn't tell that story.

"Bullshit," she said, and her incredulousness stung a little more than it should have. I shrugged like it didn't matter. I had a patent on that shrug.

"It's a matter of record," I said. "Why would I lie?"

"Why would you do half the things you do?"

"Fair point." I stepped back and took her in from top to bottom. She was even lovelier up close. Flushed and glittery. She smelled like something dark and sexy and it woke me up. Stirred my blood. "Ingrid did well. You're stunning."

My compliment had the opposite of its intended effect and she got suddenly self-conscious. She ran a hand down the sequins along her side.

"I've never worn anything so..."

Perfect.

"Loud. Don't you think it's loud?" She took a terrible risk asking me for my opinion. I could eviscerate her with one look. Not that I would, but she should know the risk. She couldn't keep walking around broadcasting all her doubt to everyone.

It was like blood in the water.

And I couldn't keep the sharks away forever.

"Ingrid knows what she's doing," I told her. "The dress is perfect."

"You have to say that," she said.

"Why?" I laughed.

"Because we're family? Kind of?" She didn't believe the words even as they came out of her mouth.

"I don't have to do anything," I said, which made her laugh and that fog of doubt around her vanished. She should always be laughing. It suited her.

The trumpeters filled the throne room with *The Herald of the King* and my father and Brenna's mother arrived on the balcony above the thrones. She wore a deep blue dress that coordinated with my father's forest-green and black uniform. It was a subtle play on the colors of our flag.

The crowd went crazy. Applause drowned out the trumpets.

We both clapped politely.

Brenna said something I couldn't hear.

"Pardon?" I asked her, leaning down so she could hear me. She shied away like I'd been about to touch her, or kiss that pink and cream spot where her neck met her shoulder.

I could see her heart pound in her throat and wondered if it was me, making that happen, or this event. Or maybe our parents up there, pretending to be in love.

I was surprised by how much I wanted it to be me.

"Do you think it's real?" she asked. The trumpeting ended and caught her yelling. She blushed, if possible, even pinker.

"Does it matter?" I asked.

"Are you going to make fun of me if I say yes?"

"I'll resist the impulse. I've heard that my parents loved each other. That when my mom was alive, things at the palace were happy. Good."

"You think it might be like that again, with our parents?" she asked, unable, un-fucking-able, to keep the hope out of her voice.

I shrugged. "What do you think?"

She sagged a little. "I think my mom wants to be queen."

"Sure, who doesn't?"

"And she doesn't want to worry about money ever again."

"Fair."

"And she's willing to do a lot for those two things."

"A business arrangement, then?"

"Something like that."

She shook her head, biting her bottom lip, the white of her teeth bright against her deep red lipstick. I suddenly wanted to pull that lip out from between her teeth with my thumb. To see, perhaps, if it was as soft as it looked.

The whole of her looked soft. And beautiful. Desirable in a sneaky, consuming kind of way.

I took a step away from her, out of reach of the subtle scent of her perfume. She even smelled soft. "So?" I asked her, making myself sharp to defend myself. "What's got you worried about a business arrangement? Marriages have been made of less." On the balcony our parents were locked in what looked like an honest and sincere kiss. "And they seem to want each other bad enough."

"I don't like the idea of my mother being hurt," she said. "It hasn't been easy for her."

It was all I could do not to gape at her. "You're worried about your mother getting hurt? She's set for life. There's no divorce for the King of Vasgar."

"And if they grow to hate each other?" she asked. "If they're locked in a loveless marriage with no respect or warmth or care?"

"Jesus," I scoffed. "You're a romantic."

"I understand why you're not," she said.

"Because it's ridiculous?"

"Because everyone knows you'll have to marry someone rich because your dad married my mom."

In Crimea, when the Russian 2B25 mortars exploded, I could feel it in my chest. Like a punch right to the ribcage but from the inside. We were a kilometer from the blast zone but my ears would ring and Alec's nose kept bleeding. It was one of those weapons that could hurt you without ever touching you.

Brenna's words were like that.

"I'm sorry," she said, honestly looking horrified. "I shouldn't have said that. I don't know why I did."

"You only said what everyone knows." I shrugged like my lungs weren't locked in a vice.

Walk away, I told myself. *Walk away. Leave her, her romance.*

But I was just so bad at walking away. And I felt, in that dark, small place inside of me, that she needed to be punished, just a little, for saying what no one said out loud.

Not to me, anyway.

"Maybe you won't have to," she said.

"Marry for money? You can't be that naive. My job is marrying the woman who will save Vasgar."

As per formal tradition, I wore gloves. They were supposed to be white, but black looked better with my uniform. They were kid leather, soft as...well, Brenna.

I touched the inside of her elbow with my fingers, a long trailing brush right over that exceedingly sensitive skin. She gasped and I waited for her to jerk away from my sinister touch. But she didn't.

And for one long heartbeat I could feel her through my fine gloves.

The throb of her pulse. The tension of her muscles.

And she didn't stay there, letting me touch her, letting me feel her, because she was worried about a scene. Or paralyzed and unsure of what to do.

She stood there, getting pinker, her breath hitching in her throat, because she wanted to be touched by me.

Well, well. This is an interesting development.

"Have a good time tonight, Brenna," I whispered near her ear. Close enough that I imagined she could smell Alec's liquor on my breath, because I could smell it on hers. "You look beautiful."

That made her jerk away, holding her arm strangely, like I'd hurt her.

I stepped out of the shadows and caught my father's eye. Brenna stepped out of the shadows behind me and beelined in some other direction, and I knew what my father was thinking, up there on the balcony.

The thunderous, disapproving look said it all.

5

THEN
Brenna

THE WEDDING WAS SCHEDULED for two weeks after the gala and I did my best to stay far away from everyone. And by everyone I meant Gunnar. That whole exchange at the gala made me uncomfortable. It was slightly terrifying how casually cruel he could be. How he weaponized his words and his touch and how easily wounded I could be by both.

He was a jerk. No doubt about it.

And he brought out the worst in me. I wasn't a fighter and I didn't want to hurt anyone. That comment I'd made about having to marry someone for money—that had been awful. And it had *hurt* him.

But really what was so damn upsetting was how, in the end, under the touch of those leather-gloved fingers, I was just like every other girl in the world he put his hands on.

Breathless.

It didn't matter that I thought he was rather loathsome, and as a member of the royal family—incredibly disappointing. His finger touched the inside of my elbow and I melted.

And he'd known it.

Really, it was just too embarrassing to even contemplate. So I did everything, absolutely everything in my power, to avoid him. Including, much to my chagrin, skipping a dance class we were supposed to take. It seemed we would be required to waltz at our parents' wedding.

Which was never going to happen.

If I had to, I would pretend to break a leg at the wedding to get out of that dance.

I did manage to get Ingrid to replace Bridget, though, and my life got a whole lot better. Ingrid at least filled me in on the gossip and made me look great for all the never-ending functions and photographs.

The nicknames in the press stopped and I became something of a nonissue.

Deiter at the *Times* actually did an interview with me. A real one. We talked in the palace library for over an hour about my thoughts and plans, and how becoming a princess was going to give me a platform I'd never had before, to help as many people as I could.

It had, I thought, gone really well. I supposed I would find out when the article was printed if Deiter had done a hatchet job on me.

And the best part? I was no longer getting lost in the castle.

Take that, doubters!

A few days before the wedding I went down for breakfast early, which usually meant that I was alone. Which was how I liked it. Me and all that coffee and the spiced rolls the chef made that I would miss like a loved one when I went back to Scotland.

My mom and the king usually came in at nine and it was a mystery when Gunnar showed up. So, when I pushed open the ornately carved doors to the family dining room at 7 a.m., imagine my shock when everyone was there.

Happy family style—the king at the head of the table. My mother at the other end. My stepbrother, the prince, sitting at a table across from an empty setting that was clearly meant for me.

We had not eaten a meal all together in private. Not once. As if we all understood deep down that we were not a family, and pretending that we were was beneath us.

But apparently not.

"We're doing *this* now?" I asked.

"Brenna!" my mom cried, looking, if I was correctly reading the rarely seen expression on her face, proud of me. She rushed over to hug me.

My mother had changed her perfume since being here. I hadn't noticed until this moment and it felt like I was hugging a stranger.

The king smiled and leaned back in his chair, and Gunnar, indifferent to me and my mother's pride, turned the page in the newspaper he was reading.

"What's going on?" I asked, patting my mom's shoulder.

"The interview," she said, keeping her arm around my shoulder, walking with me toward the table, like she used to walk me home from school. "In the *Times*?"

"Yeah?" I said cautiously. *Tell me Porky Princess didn't make another appearance. I thought it had gone so well.*

"It's so good!" Mom cried. "You sound so smart, honey."

I laughed super awkwardly. Because I was relieved and slightly stung by the "sound" part of that sentence.

"You've done the crown very proud," the king said.

"Thank you, sir."

There was literally no way to control the flop sweat and the blushing that happened when the king talked to me. And there was no way I would ever stop calling him sir. I didn't like the guy and certainly didn't respect him. But he was the king.

"Nice work, sis," Gunnar said, putting some kind of evil emphasis on *sis*, and my brain literally short-circuited with the memory of his touch on the inside of my elbow. He made it seem even more taboo.

He stood up from the table, the newspaper under his arm.

"Sit down, Gunnar," the king said. "We have something we need to discuss."

"And it has to be now?" Gunnar asked, looking at his watch.

"You have something more important to do?" the king asked.

"You have no idea, Father," Gunnar said, and Mom and I both stepped back slightly, as if hoping to get outside of blast range.

The king's salt-and-pepper beard couldn't hide the clenching of his jaw. "Sit down," he said, and there was a wild moment, fraught and explosive, when Gunnar would not sit and the king made fists on the table. And it felt like war might break out in the royal dining room.

Mom opened her mouth, like she was going to wade right into that terrible threat-filled space between the king and the prince, but I squeezed her waist, probably saving her life.

Gunnar didn't sit so much as lean against the chair, but it seemed to be enough for the king and the threat of violence was over, but it lingered a little on the hair on the back of my neck. The muscles around my knees. That space between my stomach and my heart.

How Gunnar lived like this, I couldn't even imagine.

I glanced at Mom and she smiled like she used to when I was a kid and the electricity went off in the house. *It's okay. All okay.*

That smile was a lie.

"Brenna, please sit," the king said, and I sat so fast I nearly toppled the chair. I didn't like the guy but he was still king, you know?

My mom, with far more elegance, took her spot at the foot of the table. The king pushed the article across the table toward me. "It really is impressive. I had no idea you were so interested in the political aspects of Vasgar."

"I'm interested in helping our citizens. Protecting our resources. I'm not sure how political that is."

"Everything is politics," Gunnar said.

The king spared Gunnar a glance but kept talking. "There is a royal tour of Brinmark Sound scheduled for the week following our wedding."

I looked at the king and then over at my mom. "I'm heading back to school."

"I will need you to delay your return to school for one week so you can go on the royal tour."

Need me? I thought. I didn't want that to be seductive in any way, but it was.

Vasgar needs me.

"Excellent. You can replace me!" Gunnar said hopefully.

"She will accompany you," the king said.

"What...what am I going to be doing?" I asked. "Because I really do have some ideas. I know that there's a lot of conversation about the oil rights and how there's foreign interest, but I think if we improve fisheries—"

The king started laughing. Politely, but still laughing. "It's just a tour," he said. "To show the locals that the palace is invested. And interested."

"Up until the point we sell those oil rights to Russia," Gunnar said.

The king ignored him. "You'll wave. Have your picture taken. Talk to locals. It's really very simple. But I believe, Brenna, you will be an excellent ambassador to the region."

I totally understood that the whole trip was fluff. But it was fluff in the right direction. It was a chance to inform myself and perhaps come back and inform other people. It was a chance to see right into the heart of an issue that was going to come to a crisis in my country and dictate the direction we would take.

It sounded....amazing. It sounded like the kind of work I wanted to do. Or, at least, the first step toward the work I wanted to do. "I'm in," I said. "I'm so in. I'm so super in!"

Across the table Gunnar watched me like I'd sprouted wings off my face.

And it was all I could do not to clap my hands and squeal with excitement in the face of his disinterest.

"Maybe Gunnar doesn't have to go," my mom chimed in. "I'm sure Brenna could manage—"

"I wouldn't miss it," Gunnar said. "Four days in Brinmark Sound? Perfect. Is that all?" he asked his father.

"Ann Jorgenson will be sending you everything you need."

"I love Ann!" I said, having met her at the gala.

"Of course, you do," Gunnar muttered.

"But!" Mom chimed in. "This is after the wedding. So don't get distracted."

"How could we?" Gunnar asked, and I actually laughed. The entire country had royal wedding fever and the rest of the world was catching it. Magazines and news outlets from Europe and the United States were all covering the event.

That was the power of a Cinderella story.

It was surreal being on the inside of it.

Mom smiled at me but the king had pushed away from the table. "I need to get to meetings," he said and walked around the table to kiss my mom.

"Stay out of trouble," he said to Gunnar, who only laughed. The king gave me a kind of distracted smile and then he was gone.

"I need to meet the dressmaker," Mom said, and then she, too, was gone, out a different door. Leaving me and Gunnar and a sudden explosion of butterflies in my stomach. I stood up and grabbed a cup of coffee from the buffet behind me.

"You should try one of those spiced rolls," Gunnar said. "They're really good."

I closed my eyes and blew out a long breath, pushing as hard as I could. "Don't you have to be somewhere?"

"Like where?"

"A bar?"

"It's not even 9 a.m., Brenna," he said in that smooth voice. I didn't have to look at him to know he'd be sprawled across some chair, grinning at me like he was a cat and I was a mouse he couldn't wait to torture. "What kind of man do you think I am?"

"A bad one," I said with a dry chuckle that sounded meaner than I intended.

I turned and he wasn't sitting in his chair like the ruined prince of a kingdom he didn't much like. Instead, he was standing right behind me. Close enough I startled, sloshing coffee onto the floor.

"What are you doing?"

"You skipped the dance lesson."

I laughed. "Like you care."

"I do care."

"Did you even go?"

He nodded.

"Well, we're not going to need that dance class," I said.

"You can waltz?"

"No. But it doesn't matter. We're not going to waltz."

"It is required. It's literally a law."

"Stop it." I laughed.

"You think I'm joking? They could hang you for treason."

"For not dancing with you?"

He shrugged. "I don't make the laws."

"You will someday," I said, suddenly sober. "You'll be part of the government that rules this country."

"What does that have to do with our waltz?"

"Nothing," I said quietly. "But it has a lot to do with Brinmark Sound."

He stepped back and that hungry cat look on his face froze right over.

"I'm sorry," I said. "If I'm intruding on a thing you are invested—"

"I don't give a shit about the Sound," he said, and this time it was my expression freezing.

"No," I said. "Of course not."

I took my cup of coffee and walked away, leaving the spice rolls behind, much to my dismay.

"Waltz practice," he yelled at me. "Today at two in the ballroom. Don't be late."

I wondered if it would be a princessly thing to do to give

him the finger as I left the royal dining room. And then I decided I didn't care and did it anyway.

The door shut on the sound of his laughter.

Gunnar

I GOT Ingrid to help us with the waltz; that she brought Alec with her was a surprise.

"You guys are back on?" I asked, stepping into the giant empty ballroom. The floor was jade and marble tiles, and all the fixtures were the pink-hued stone from our northern beaches. It was an exceedingly feminine room. And really kind of pretty. The windows looked out on the rocky shore at the end of the gardens. It was nothing but the North Sea up there. And today was one of those September days—bright and clear. Quiet. Looking out the window you'd never guess we were on the top edge of the world.

"No," Ingrid said, at the same time Alec said, "Yes!"

"Alec," Ingrid sighed. "We talked about this."

"You talked. I didn't agree."

Ingrid was about to get outraged, but the door opened and Brenna walked in looking like she was being marched to her death.

"What?" she said to me, and I realized I was staring at her. She was wearing the dress she'd worn when I first met her. The yellow sundress that made her look like summer on the outer islands. She wore her bright red shoes with it and I couldn't lie—she looked fucking hot.

The thought was a sudden one. And a comfortable one. Easy, even. It helped me put her in a box I recognized. Beautiful girl I'd like to sleep with. That was a well-used box in my life. It was, in fact, a central theme in my life. I took a deep breath and felt my shoulders lower about an inch.

There was no box for Brenna otherwise. No easy category for her.

"Glad you came," I said, smiling at her.

She narrowed her eyes at me and I found that hot, too.

"Are we ready for some waltzing?" Ingrid asked, clapping her hands.

"Not really," Brenna said. "No."

"We're going to do this crash-course style," Ingrid said. "Just enough so you don't run into anything on the dance floor and there are no pictures of you two tripping over each other in the *Times* the next morning."

"Well," Brenna said. "That doesn't sound too bad."

"Waltzing is easy," I said, and Alec's booming laugh echoed off the marble floors and pillars. We all winced.

"It's hard," Alec said. "Super hard. You've got to do ten things at once."

"I think she can handle it," I said, and Brenna looked at me quickly and then away.

"Let's just do this," she said. "Is there music or what?"

"You guys will be dancing to the Shostakovich 'Waltz No. 2,'" Ingrid said and pointed at Alec who pressed a button on his phone. The chamber echoed with classical music that had a familiar waltz tempo but at the same time sounded... haunting and completely different.

I loved everything about it.

"Really?" Brenna asked. "This?"

Ingrid shrugged and pointed at me. "He picked it."

"You?" she asked.

"Why is that surprising?" I asked, but I knew. I knew exactly why it was surprising. Because she'd put me in a box, too, and I wasn't staying in it.

How distressing for her. I'd found a box she could stay in and I kept crawling out of the one she wanted me in.

All of this made me feel better.

"Come on," I said. "Let's get going. I've got things to do."

She snorted as she walked across the ballroom. The hem of that yellow skirt ruffled around her knees. "Like what?" She came to stop in front of me, her hands on her hips. She had frown lines between her eyes, like she was thinking really mean things about me.

"An ab set with my trainer."

Oh, she rolled her eyes so hard, I was surprised she didn't pass out. And then she held up her arms like she was impersonating a cactus.

"Are you kidding?"

"What do you mean?"

"What am I supposed to do with you?" I touched the tips of her fingers, which, at contact, curled into a fist. "Hang clothes on you?"

"Stop."

I touched her elbow and she flinched away.

"Seriously," she said. "Stop."

When I stepped toward her she stepped back, eyeing me like I was about to steal her purse.

All in all, I loved it. Because I knew exactly what to do with her discomfort.

Grow it.

"Brenna," I said, slowly. "It's a waltz. I have to touch you."

"Yeah, I know, but..." She looked at Ingrid and Alec, who were watching us with a kind of dawning horror on Alec's part and delight on Ingrid's. Finally, Brenna took a deep breath. "Okay. Fine. Touch me."

Oh, god, she was too easy. Too delicious.

I stepped toward her and watched as she battled herself

to stay where she was. To keep her footing. "You want to run," I murmured, sliding my hand around her waist.

She flinched, but stood there. "I want to punch your nose."

"Come on." I smiled at her, gathering her hand in mine. "Relax."

"I am. I'm totally calm."

"Your palms are sweating."

"You're the worst."

"Probably," I sighed, smiling into her flushed face. Her body was warm. And I pulled her closer, until her belly touched mine. She sucked in a breath and held it, and I felt her trembling against me.

My own breath stalled in my throat. A strange solid lump.

"So?" she whispered and then cleared her throat. "What do we do now?"

"Get a room," Alec said, and Ingrid smacked him in the shoulder.

"Start the music over," I said. Brenna's blue eyes were wide and unblinking. Despite blue eyes and blond hair being literally the most common combination in my country, I found myself thinking about the uniqueness of her hair and her eyes and her darker eyebrows.

It felt like I'd never seen that combination before. That it was entirely rare.

She was entirely rare.

The music restarted and I counted out the steps and the rhythm. "One two three," I whispered, turning her slowly, leading her in circles around the dance floor.

She stumbled and we stalled.

"You're trying to lead me," I told her.

"I don't know what you're talking about."

"There can only be one person in charge in a waltz."

"Then we should decide now, shouldn't we?" she asked. "Who is in charge."

I smiled at her, felt the laughter rolling up from my stomach.

"Sweetheart," I whispered. "In this, I am always in charge."

The words came out loaded and a little naughty, and Brenna's dark eyebrows crashed together. A storm cloud indicating her shift in mood.

Perversely, I found it...intriguing. I was quite used to women being angry with me, but there was something so different about her anger. I lapped it up. Teased more of it out of her because the crackle and pop of her temper tasted so sweet to me.

"Would you like to be in charge of other things?" I asked.

"Don't be an ass."

Distracted she was a better dancer, but I didn't say that, because I could feel her wanting to slap me and leave. And we really did need to do this. "I'm glad you're going to the coast with me," I said, spinning her a little faster. The pace of our dancing finally matched the tempo of the song.

"No, you're not."

"Of course I am. You can do all the work. That's what you can be in charge of. The work."

"Does it really mean nothing to you?" she asked. "That the future of our kingdom will be decided in the Sound? Is it all such a joke?"

For a moment, I wanted to protest that of course it wasn't. Because I wasn't such an ass that I couldn't see that it was important. I was aware of it being important. But all I'd shown her was my indifference.

Because that was all I had. All I was allowed.

She took my silence as an answer she liked and her hand clenched mine. "We have power," she said. "I don't know what it is, yet. But we have some. We can change things."

I stepped back. Dropped my arms from her body. Felt something cold and stiff in my brain. "You've been here for all of a minute," I said. "You have no idea what you're talking about."

"It's because I've been here a minute that I can see things a little clearer," she said and stepped up closer to me.

"You live in Scotland. What do you think you can actually accomplish?"

She smiled, wide and bright. "Anything."

Oh, god. That hope was exhausting. And ridiculous.

I turned back to Alec and Ingrid who watched us with their mouths agape. "What do you think?"

"I think you shouldn't fight on the dance floor," Ingrid said.

"And you probably shouldn't fuck," Alec added.

"I don't think that will be a problem," I said with some casual cruelty thrown into the mix. "Do you?"

Brenna looked at me, disappointed and taken aback.

That is how you learn, I thought. That is how it is taught at the royal palace. Do not care because you will be mocked for it. Your hand, as you reach for things, will be slapped and slapped again until you just stop reaching.

"Are we done?" she asked.

"Ingrid?" I asked, not looking away from Brenna and her uniqueness all lit up with her anger. With her frustration and maybe disgust of me.

It made me want to touch her again, because she might be disgusted by me, but I could make her want me. I could make her lips part on a bated breath. I could make her eyes go wide and her heart pound against that tender place in her neck.

Yeah. She might hate me, but she was always going to be one touch away from wanting me. And I could see in her eyes that she knew it, too.

And she hated it.

"I think you'll be all right," Ingrid said, as though from a million miles away.

"We'll be all right," I said, tasting the words. Testing them. Wondering if they were true or if we were on a collision course, the two of us, with something big and powerful and far, far outside of my control.

Brenna, with her unreachable, unreadable face, nodded once, just once. And walked away.

6

T HEN
Brenna

I WATCHED my mom get married in a silk wedding dress with a twenty-foot lace train. I watched a tear slip from the corner of her eye and didn't even wonder if it was real or not.

Because all I could think was: I am a princess now. I mean...holy shit. I'm a fucking princess.

Was that the kind of thing I could get on my driver's license?

I was my mother's attendant and she'd chosen a bright green dress for me, a filmy thing that required basically a scuba-suit foundation garment. But it made my eyes look like the ice on Fasso Lake.

The wedding wasn't terrible, much to my surprise. It was lovely, really. As intimate as possible with over five hundred guests. Almost all of them strangers. Dignitaries from foreign countries. The council members and their extended families.

But the church was beautiful, way out on the cliffs. The reception was in a tent on the great expanse of grass between the church and the castle. There were Vasgar flags flying from every corner and turret, and they fluttered in a cool breeze that came in off the water.

Mom and I wore white fur capes, and three weeks ago I'd though the capes were ridiculous. But the weather changed so fast way up here on the edge of the North Island and I was grateful for mine today.

My Aunt Olivia was there, and my cousin Edda came from Edinburgh, but I'd lost them in the official rules and proceedings of the ceremony. But under the tent of the reception, I ducked around, through, and past people I didn't know until I spotted Edda's beautiful chestnut curls.

"You look beautiful!" Edda said, wrapping me in her arms and the smell of clove cigarettes and the changing weather and far-off places. Edda always smelled that way. Even as a girl, she'd smelled like change. Like someone heading for the horizon. I envied that about her more than I could say.

"Thank you," I said.

"You're a right fucking princess now!"

"I am!" I laughed because she wanted me to laugh. "I am a right fucking princess."

"I can't believe it."

"Trust me. Neither can I."

I pulled out of her arms so I could take her in. She wore a dress made of some silver material and a Scottish tartan. Her father's clan. "You look like a proper Scot."

And a knockout. Edda was a total knockout. *She* could

wear a black bag and she'd be the most stunning person in the room.

"I am," she said. "And I need a drink."

She tucked her arm in mine and we walked away from the hundreds of people I didn't know and didn't particularly care to know. "Tell me everything," she said.

"There's not that much to tell, really," I said. "It's been fine. Busy. How are my plants?"

"Very dead."

"Edda!"

"Kidding. They're fine. Mostly. Your mom is okay?"

"Happy."

"Really?"

I shrugged. "I don't know if it's the kind of happy that will last."

"It rarely is for our moms, is it? What about you?"

"What about me?"

Edda plucked two glasses of champagne off a tray as a waiter walked by. She handed one to me. I wanted to download all of it. I wanted to vent and open up my soul and just let it all come pouring out. The poison and the pleasure. I wanted to get a little drunk and tell my cousin everything.

But I was a princess now and it didn't seem...right. If I'd learned anything the last few weeks, it was that the facade was all that mattered. A drunk princess would be a problem.

"I shouldn't..."

"You one hundred percent should," she said.

There were no photographers at the reception. The wedding had been televised in three different countries. But the reception was private and no one was going to take a bunch of pictures of the now princess drinking champagne.

"You're right," I said, and I downed the glass. "Get two more. Let's find a place to sit."

Edda lifted her eyebrows and the fun was on. Oh, that giggly, wild look in her eye, I knew it well. It was the look that had made me feel better in the dark days back home. We had both been raised by single moms who hadn't quite gotten the lives they wanted.

Well, I thought, looking at my mom as a beautiful bride at the entrance of the tent. That wasn't true anymore.

"Holy shit," I breathed. "My mom is a queen."

Edda howled, said something to one of the waiters, and soon we had our own bottle of champagne and a table in the corner where we could drink it. The reception seemed to swirl around without us and one bottle of champagne turned into two and a tray of the crab canapés.

"You sound excited about that trip to Brinmark Sound."

"I am. I am so excited. It's...all a show. I know. But still, I get to talk to people. Find out what they need, how they can be helped."

"You are too good for this place, Brenna."

"I don't know about that." I was drunk and talking to Edda, a person I trusted with my soul, so I felt safe saying the thing out loud I'd only just started to believe in. "Maybe I can help this place be better. Serve the kingdom the way it should be."

"What about the UN?"

"Why can't I do both?"

"Always the optimist," Edda said. "Tell me about the prince."

"The who?"

"The prince!" she whisper yelled.

"He's the worst," I said. But suddenly, from the bottom of two bottles of champagne, I couldn't say if that was actually true or not. "I think. Maybe. Maybe not?"

And I tried, I really did, to make everything that the

prince was clear to my cousin. And to myself. Gunnar was an asshole, yes. But parts of him were kind. And parts of him were curious. And it seemed—sometimes—he wanted to do the right thing.

Sometimes.

Suddenly the seat to my left was no longer empty. Gunnar sat there, in his elegant black uniform with the red-and-white trim.

"Speak of the devil," I said.

Edda, who in the fifth grade had punched William Fitzroy in the nose for telling people that she'd let him touch her boob, was staring agog at Gunnar beside me.

"Were you just talking about me?" Gunnar asked.

"Yes," I said.

"Saying only nice things, I assume," he said, his lush mouth all kinds of smiley. God, he had an amazing mouth. Even when he smirked, I sorta wanted to kiss him.

"Not really." I lifted my champagne glass, disappointed to find it empty. "We need more champagne."

"Perhaps you'd care to introduce me, Brenna," he said in that voice that was just stuffed full of laughter. That voice was a weird trick, because there were times when the laughter inside that voice was at me.

And sometimes it was with me. Or for me. *Or* something much more kind. And human.

"Oh, I think you've met plenty of champagne."

"Oh, my god," Edda whispered. "He means to me. Introduce him to me."

Whoops. Right.

"Edda, this is Prince Gunnar. He's a bit of a dick, but everyone lets him get away with it because he's really good-looking." I swiveled in my chair. "And Gunnar, this is my very favorite person in the world—my cousin Edda. So don't be mean. And don't sleep with her, either. I don't think that would be a good idea."

"Lovely to meet you, Edda," he said. "I suppose we're family now."

"I never thought of it that way," Edda said.

Prince Gunnar said something in the old language, about his home being her home.

"That's sweet," I said. "You're not so bad." I turned to my cousin. "Edda, he's not so bad." I whispered that to her because I'd been telling her Gunnar was pretty bad.

Edda put her face in her hands and Gunnar lifted a bottle of champagne.

"Oh, would you like some?" I asked. Thinking maybe if Gunnar and I had a drink, we could let down all the weapons we'd formed against each other. Maybe we could have a drink, lay down our weapons and have a laugh.

Get to know each other.

"I think you drank it all, Brenna," he said with a smile that had no sharpness. Was only soft. I smiled back at him.

"That's too bad," I said. "We should get more."

"Lovely idea," he said. "But first, let's dance."

I flopped back in my chair like a three-year-old at the beginning of a tantrum. "I don't want to."

"Brenna," Edda said. Trying I could tell to be a voice of reason. "I think you're supposed to."

"Ugh. So much supposed to. I don't like it," I told them both. "I really don't."

"How about this, Brenna," he said. "Let's go do our dance. And then you and your cousin can join Alec and Ingrid and me with a few other friends in my quarters for a party."

"But we're already at a party," I said, and he gave me

what I was coming to see as his *oh, Brenna, you poor fool* look. I didn't like that look.

"We can be at a better party. Come," he said and stood, his hand out toward me. I wanted him, all of a sudden, to say something nice to me in the old language. To tell me that his home was my home. Or to say the same thing his father had said to my mother—that I was his to protect and care for.

I didn't like thinking that, but the thoughts were there nonetheless. I wanted this reckless miscreant with his gray eyes and dark power over me to like me. When I wasn't all that sure I liked him. Mostly I didn't.

But this was familiar territory. I was used to wanting something from the people in my life that they weren't willing or able to give.

"Brenna," he said with a softer smile. "They're expecting us. It's time for us to waltz."

"Right!" I said, clapping my hands and getting to my feet. Edda and Gunnar both propped me up when I wobbled. I'd gotten hot drinking all that champagne and long ago had ditched the cape so Gunnar's hand on my bare skin was warm and smooth and...electric.

I looked at him, his hand still on me, and it felt like a current ran between us, between his hand and my skin and his dark eyes and mine.

"Uh-oh," I heard Edda, say but Gunnar was leading me off toward the dance floor where the lighting changed and the orchestra was silent for a moment.

The king with his loud king voice said, "I introduce Prince Gunnar of Vasgar and my new daughter—Princess Brenna."

Gunnar put his hand on my waist and I put my suddenly sweating palm on his shoulder, and the music lifted us up in its swell. And suddenly we were dancing. He held me a little farther away than he had during practice, but I knew at practice he'd only been trying to provoke me. This time, under the lights that weren't spotlights but felt a little like they were, he held me stiffly. Formally.

"Did you hear?" I said.

"What?"

"I'm a princess now."

He smiled, wide and bright, showing his teeth, even. A beautiful smile—ungoverned and real and one I'd never seen. One I'd never imagined he was capable of. But then it was gone. His face once again slipped into a careful, distant expression.

"I heard."

I smiled. "You hate this," I said.

"So much."

I smiled harder.

"You shouldn't do that," he said.

"Do what?"

"Smile."

"Is it forbidden now that I'm a princess? We all have to walk around like you?" I tried to mimic his expression, not his blank face of the moment. But that expression he usually wore, the sparkly leer. The conspiratorial, sexy smirk.

"That's your impression of me?" he asked, and he was laughing and I was laughing. And the whispering crowd in the shadows on the edge of the dance floor fell away.

"Pretty good, right?"

He scrunched up his face and rolled his eyes.

"Is that me?" I cried.

"Totally you." He rolled his eyes again for good measure.

The song was ending and we were whirling faster and I had no idea I could dance like this and it suddenly occurred to me that it took being drunk—and it took Gunnar—to bring out this side of me. And I didn't hate this side of me.

"Not everything has to be so serious," I said.

"Amen, sister."

"Literally." I laughed and then so did he.

"Do we have to hate each other?" I asked.

"I don't hate you, Brenna," he said. "But whatever you feel about me right now, it's not entirely real."

"I think I'm capable of knowing my own feelings. And I feel friendly, Gunnar. Towards you."

"You feel drunk."

"What did I say about being from South Island?"

"Well, tomorrow, instead of checking the traps, you're going to wake up and remember you don't like me."

"But I do," I said, and it was strange. My tone was strange. My voice. I sounded worried. I sounded slightly scared and terribly, terribly honest.

His eyes on mine were wide. And I'd managed to surprise the prince.

The music ended and he stopped, my skirts twirling around us and then he dipped me. Something we hadn't practiced. Something I'd never done. And I shrieked and dropped his hand to grab his shoulder.

I was clinging to him, laughing up at his painfully handsome face. The applause all around us. And all at once my heart was in my throat and my stomach was near my feet and he was so much more than I'd thought he was. He was surprising in every way.

He didn't lift me up, and we stood there, my weight in his strong arms. Our laughter changing into something else. Something breathless and electric.

I wanted to kiss him. Or I wanted him to kiss me.

"Brenna," he whispered. "We can't—"

I realized I was leaning up to do it. In front of all these people I was trying to kiss him!

My entire body flinched.

Suddenly the lights on us flashed off and new music was playing. Gunnar lifted me to my feet and I stumbled a little, light-headed and clumsy.

"Are you all right?" he asked.

"I'm fine. I'm..." Drunk. Confused. Suddenly worried.

"You didn't do anything wrong," he said, proving he could somehow read my mind. "Remember that."

His arm still around my waist he led me to the side of the dance floor. Where my cousin was waiting for me. The king seemed to come out of nowhere and took Gunnar by the elbow, leading him off into the shadows.

"Your mom is coming," Edda said. "Let's go."

Edda pulled me away from the edge of the dance floor, deeper into the shadows of the party, and I stumbled along with her, aware somehow that something had changed.

7

T HEN
Gunnar

THE LAND out by the Sound was some of the most beautiful in my country. Steep cliffs blanketed by green trees, falling, it seemed, into water so clear and cold and deep it was black. The sky an almost constant grey, broken by miraculous days of sunshine.

Brinmark Sound was surrounded by ancient lands with burial grounds and ruins. Most of our people still believed there was magic here.

The royal visit to the Sound was graced with the kinds of days that made you believe the old myths. All week long Brenna and I accepted wreaths and bouquets and listened to kids sing us songs in the old language. And the sun was so bright and the land so beautiful our eyes teared.

On our last day I stood at the rail of one of the area tour

boats that made trips around the Sound. Today it had been commandeered to take us to its far edges.

With the Russian survey ship in the distance.

It suddenly very much bothered me. That Russian survey ship. A blight on a perfect landscape.

The mayor, Vera Wilkinson, was sharp in every way. I was not surprised to find out she was a cousin of Ann Jorgenson. Her conversation got right to the point and she spent no time blowing smoke up my ass. Which put me off balance. I wasn't used to people speaking frankly to me.

And it was obvious she did not like my father.

"Your father has plans to open all this territory to foreign oil companies," she said, pointing out at that survey ship like it was proof. And the more I looked at it, the more it seemed true.

Brenna stood on the other side of her, soaking up every word.

"I wouldn't say they were plans," I hedged. Because, so far, the council had blocked him and Vasgar didn't have enough money that we could start drilling on our own.

"The Russians paid to send that survey ship and I'm guessing that money went right into the royal wedding," Vera said with a powerfully dismissive sniff.

I wished to god I could argue. Brenna and I shared a guilty glance, because for sure that was true. Last week we'd drunk hundred-dollar-a-bottle champagne and today we'd met families struggling to put meat on the table.

My privilege turned rancid and sour in my stomach.

"But you can't argue with the fact that foreign oil companies would bring quite a bit of money to this region," I said, falling back on what I'd heard my father say over and over again. "Money for schools, infrastructure."

All things this area desperately needed. The schools

we'd visited were practically still heated by wood-burning stoves.

"Foreign investment, yes. Absolutely," the mayor said. "Foreign *control* we have to fight, Your Highness."

"Tell us what the distinction is, in your eyes," Brenna said. She'd been like that the whole trip, asking the mayor her opinion. Asking the mayor to be extremely clear about what she thought and what she wanted. It had been exceedingly helpful.

Brenna had been exceedingly helpful.

"Foreign control means the Russians could drill for oil with no regard to the protection and care of this environment. The protection and care of this community. Jobs, good paying and highly skilled, would go to the citizens of another country, when this area right here needs those jobs. Foreign investment still gives us control."

"There would be jobs no matter what," I said.

"Yes, and the difference between working on the rig and working in the bar that serves the men who work on the rig is the difference that could change this country forever."

Man, that put the whole thing into perspective.

The mayor stepped back and Brenna and I both turned to face her. She was so small, the mayor. And so strong. I wished, all of a sudden, that I could have an answer for her. That I could put her mind at ease.

I wished that I could do the right thing. The strange newness of that feeling made me step back, brace myself against the railing of the boat.

"Selling our oil rights," Vera said, "will be the same pillaging our country has always suffered at the hands of invaders."

"Your point is very well made," Brenna said, and I could see that she was convinced. Hell. I was convinced. But I hated to break it to Brenna. If I had very little power, she had none.

"Your mother was from this part of the country," the mayor said, her eyes practically poking holes in my head.

"I know," I said, and I knew what she would say before the words came out of her mouth.

"And she would want you to protect her homeland."

"Thank you, mayor," I said, dismissing her because I couldn't take any more. Her righteous desire to do right by this land and the people. And my inability to offer her any hope that the royal family would be able to help her. Vera bowed and headed back toward the warmer part of the boat. I expected Brenna to follow but she stayed right at the railing.

I took a deep breath and stared at the water going by, the blue-green ribbons covered in white froth.

"I didn't know your mother was from here," Brenna said.

"Ingla," I said. The biggest city about twenty miles inland.

"The mayor makes a good point."

I nodded. "But you haven't heard the other side. They make good points, too. About the country being bankrupt and how the selling of the oil rights will settle all of our debts as well as give us the opportunity to improve schools, hospitals, roads...everything."

"Foreign investment won't do that?"

"I don't know." I didn't have to tell her that I'd stayed out of politics. That I'd stayed out of everything but gossip magazines and the beds of beautiful women. She was plenty aware.

I wasn't ashamed of anything. I wasn't born for shame. Or regret. But something sat uncomfortably in the pit of my stomach.

This was something I should know.

"Well," she said. "Let's find out."

I laughed. "Good idea."

Brenna didn't say anything more. But neither did she leave. And in the wind-whipped silence between us, the tension cranked up. And then up again.

If she had been any other girl, I'd have taken her by the hand and found the closest room with a lock so we could get this out of our systems.

But she wasn't any other girl. She was Brenna. The Royal Princess.

My stepsister.

And completely off limits.

"It's so pretty," she said.

It was hard not looking at her. Everything in me wanted to turn sideways, smile at her, watch the wind make a mess of her hair. Tease her until her neck went red.

But Father had made it clear. And for once he wasn't wrong. And for once I was going to listen.

I had to stay away from Brenna.

"It is," I said.

"I've never been here. I mean, this far north."

She'd been carrying a guidebook with her the whole time. Reading aloud the historical facts to anyone who would listen. I knew more about the fishing industry in Brinmark Sound than I'd ever wanted to know. And the impact of the Vikings.

Foreign invaders who had pillaged this land for hundreds of years. I looked back out at that Russian survey ship.

"Are you ignoring me?"

Yes. But I shook my head. "No."

"Seems like it."

I imagined it did. But for the first time in a long time, I didn't know what to do with a particular woman.

That box I'd put her in was smashed. Because, yes, I wanted to sleep with her. But I also wanted to talk to her about this Russian investment business. And I wanted to see her smile. And make her laugh. I wanted to get her drunk again and waltz all night long.

There was no box for all of those things.

"I'm sorry," she said in a wild rush, like she'd been storing up the words. "About the wedding and the dance. I was drunk—"

"You didn't do anything," I said and finally forced myself to look at her. Oh, god, she was agonized and probably had been since the minute I left her on the side of that dance floor. "Really. Brenna. You didn't do anything." Not that my father or her mother saw it that way.

It would be easy, painfully easy, to sharpen some offhand joke to a razor's edge and scrape it against that soft heart she wore so insistently on her sleeve. Something cruel and dismissive that would push her firmly away.

So easy.

But I swallowed all those simple barbs. Because sometimes burning down the world was excessive, despite how much I liked it.

"Brenna," I said, and I even smiled at her, to soften, perhaps, the awkwardness of this conversation. To turn us from...whatever we were...into friends of a sort. "You very nearly kissed me on that dance floor."

Predictably her face went red, her eyes immediately trained on the landscape slipping by the side of our boat, though I could tell she wasn't seeing much of it.

"I'm so embarrassed," she said.

"Don't be. You were drunk. And I'm a man women want

to kiss." She shot me a sideways eye roll and I stepped marginally closer. "And the truth is," I told her. "I would have kissed you back."

"Don't—" she whispered and put her hand up once before curling it into a fist.

"Don't what?"

"Don't lie."

Oh, god. Why was she making this so difficult? Why was I suddenly consumed with musical montages of showing her just how lovely she was? How desirable with those thundercloud eyes and lush body. I could make her believe. I could convince her of her appeal and her desirability in such a way that she could never again be convinced otherwise.

Fuck. That would be fun.

But as my father had told me—Brenna was not one of my playthings.

So instead all I said was, "You're lovely, Brenna."

Predictably, she shook off the words.

And that right there was my tipping point. The collision course we'd been on since she walked into the royal hall a month ago.

What was the point of having this reputation if I didn't make use of it? Didn't take full advantage?

She was off to Scotland in literally days and I wanted this. Wanted her. With all her contradictions. And I was terrible at restraint.

So I would have her. Just a little. Enough to put this chemistry away.

This decision, once made, was a goddamned relief.

I grabbed her hand and pulled her to the front of the boat. I pushed open the door to the small viewing cabin they must use in bad weather. The door shut behind us and the big empty room echoed with the slam of the door.

"What...what are you doing?"

I turned her to face me, her cheeks pink, her eyes narrowed. God, I loved that. Turned on and suspicious all at the same time. How purely Brenna.

"What do you think I'm doing?" I asked, walking toward her, and she predictably stepped back. Again and again, until I had her in the corner of the cabin. No one could see us unless they looked in through the front window and there was nothing there but ocean.

"Gunnar." Her back against the wall, she put her hand on my chest.

"Brenna." I picked up that hand on my chest, kissed the palm of it. She gasped—adorably—and I put her hand around my neck.

"This...what...?"

"You're very smart, Brenna. Maybe the smartest person I know. Surely you can guess what is about to happen."

"You're going to kiss me."

"I am." I smiled down at her, suddenly very excited about the prospect. Perhaps too excited. I shifted backward the hips I'd been using to crowd her against the metal corner of the room.

"Why?"

"Why what?"

"I mean...is this a joke? Or some awful bet—"

I pressed my thumb against that lush bottom lip of hers. She made one squeaking sound and then shut up. The only sound the panting of her breath over my finger.

"I'm going to kiss you because I'm done pretending I don't want to. I'm going to kiss you because this lower lip of yours is positively begging for it. I'm going to kiss you because thinking about it and not doing it has started to make me crazy."

"Crazy?"

"Yes, Brenna. Out of my mind." I was leaning down as I said this, my forearms braced on the wall over her head. I don't know how she managed to mess with time, but I felt like I'd been wanting to kiss her for ages. Weeks. A year maybe?

And I'd known her all of a month.

Our lips touched, a feather-soft glance, and she gasped. I gasped?

And her hand around my neck pulled me closer and closer still until there was nothing featherlight about this kiss. It was warm and wet, and her soft body, buried beneath the tweed coat she wore, was in my arms. She licked at me, her tongue against my lips, and I groaned in my throat.

My plan, pulling her in here had been so clear. A kiss and then a promise we couldn't do this again. That we couldn't. It would be a kiss to satisfy an itch and then it would be over.

Truthfully, perhaps part of me thought that it would be awful. She was young and green, perhaps a virgin. I had low expectations for the impact of this kiss. I was, after all, the notorious Prince Gunnar of Vasgar.

But here I was, groaning in my throat, pushing her up against the wall, my tongue in her mouth. She pulled at my hair, her legs restless against mine and this kiss...this kiss was no longer a kiss. It was the beginning of something.

Of trouble.

"Gunnar," she gasped, digging through my coat.

"Yes," I hissed. Honestly, had I really thought I could kiss her and not touch her? I'd been thinking about her body every minute of every day since she burst into my life in that yellow dress. I dropped my arm from the wall above her head and pulled open the tie on her coat, finding her beneath it. The smooth fabric of whatever dress she was wearing and, under that, the warmth of her. The give and push of her.

My heartbeat was pounding in my cock and everything in my head was telling me to ease myself against her. To find some kind of relief in the friction of her body against mine. But I stopped myself. I did. Because this was already far too dangerous. We were doused in kerosene and carrying matches.

But I slipped my hand between her coat and her dress, curving it around her waist with increasing pressure, squeezing her until my palm was on her ass.

She moaned against my mouth. Needy little thing. Aching, probably, just like I was.

A thousand dirty questions battered at my lips. I wanted to make her beg. I wanted her to tell me—with eyes wide open and cheeks on fire with a blush—exactly what she wanted me to do to her.

I palmed her ass. Squeezed it.

And the want, the desire I had been living with and denying and fighting exploded inside of me. The point of no return was now. Here. It was stop or fuck her against this wall.

I stepped back. And then again. And still it wasn't enough. I turned away until I couldn't see her, not even out of the corner of my eye. But it took a long time until I could breathe.

"That—" was all I said. No idea how I intended to finish that sentence. Was awesome? Surprising? A terrible mistake?

"I know," she said.

I glanced at her over my shoulder and with one look I could see she was feeling exactly the same thing. Regret and surprise and a long slow worry that we'd opened Pandora's box and we'd never, ever get it closed again.

"It's a very inconvenient chemistry we have, Brenna."

"So, what do we do?" she asked. She was still leaning against that wall. Her jacket a tangle around her. Her green dress twisted around her body. Her hair a mess where apparently, I'd been gripping it in my hands.

Fuck.

I took a deep breath of the cold, briny air. "Nothing."

"What?"

How strange to be the reasonable one, but someone had to be.

I turned back to face her and I held my arms out wide.

"Nothing can happen between us, Brenna. My father is wrong about so many things, but he's right about that. It would be a scandal the royal family would never live down. It would ruin me, which isn't a very big deal considering how close to ruin I already am—"

"Gunnar—"

"Brenna," I said, emphatic and cold. "As bad as it might be for me. It will be a million times worse for you. If I get ruined you would be..." I hated even thinking about it. That awful double standard that would treat her so much more harshly than it would ever treat me. "Destroyed."

"I don't live here, remember?" But I wasn't sure if she was trying to convince me that she would survive, or just reminding both of us that the country and life of the royal family was not for her.

"You don't think the news that you slept with your step-brother the prince would follow you? Because it would. The world is small for royal families."

"So, we just ignore each other."

"We don't have to ignore each other," I said. "We just have to ignore this." I waved my hands between us, my coat and scarf flapping.

"Are you suggesting we become...friends?" Her kiss-ravaged mouth was smiling at me.

I looked out the window at the seagulls arcing through the bright blue sky because looking at her was too awkward. "I've never been very good with friends."

"Ingrid?"

"She does all the hard work. And she's always been in love with Alec."

Brenna laughed. "You're saying you've managed to be friends with her because she's never fallen for you?"

I shrugged, feeling my cheeks get hot.

"I suppose that explains Alec, too?"

"I'm friends with Alec because he doesn't go away."

"And who doesn't love Alec?"

"Exactly."

"I'm very good with friends," she said with that starchy pride she had. She pushed herself off the wall and straightened her coat and then her hair. Like I'd never touched her.

"Wonderful. You can lead me in this."

She smiled at me, revealing her bright white teeth, the small gap between the front two that I found somehow...erotic.

But that thought was not in the spirit of friendship, so I pushed it away.

"Friends," she said and held out her gloved hand.

"Friends," I said and shook it.

Both of us ignored the wild zap of electricity. The sudden painful curiosity that simmered beneath our kidskin gloves, the urge to feel more. Know more.

There on the edge of that boat, on the edge of our kingdom and what seemed like the world, we smiled at each other and it felt like something new was starting in my life. That the seeds that were planted when she walked into the palace weeks ago were blossoming.

And I promised myself I was not going to ruin it.

Next week she'd be back in Scotland.

8

N OW
New York City
Brenna

IN THE BASEMENT of that seedy club, I lifted my arm. With the champagne flute in my hand, my fingers almost... almost touched Gunnar's chest. Maybe that was my plan. Maybe it wasn't. I could hardly be sure in this wild moment.

"To King Gunnar. Long live the king."

Gunnar snarled, grabbed my arm, and all but dragged me across the marble floor to a closed door set in the opposite wall. I was, in that moment, his hand gripping my elbow, so glad for the cashmere and the fur.

I could not feel him. Not at all.

Though I could smell him. Whiskey and cologne and, beneath that, him. The smell of Gunnar that had seeped into my skin and bones years ago. I could outrun a lot of things, burn the memories of him to ash, but the smell of him...that I could not ignore. And it went through me like a spear.

He opened the door, hustled me into a small office, and slammed the door behind us. The office...this space I recognized. While that outer room might be for show, like any good throne room, this room was all Gunnar. Wood walls, bookshelves. A leather couch. A desk covered in coffee cups and notebooks. An old-fashioned turntable in the corner, surrounded by records.

Records everywhere.

The dam trembled, but I sniffed and put my back to the music and the memories, facing Gunnar like our history wasn't breathing down my neck.

"What happened?" he asked.

"Heart attack," I said. "If you'd answered any of the emails or calls you'd know he'd been sick for a while."

"How is your mother?" he asked, surprising me.

"Fine."

He smiled...or sneered? It was hard to tell with him.

"And you?" he asked.

"Also fine."

"Why are you lying?"

"Because I will never again give you a weapon to use against me, Gunnar."

The words came out unbidden, cracking in the air like ice in spring. I had not meant to say that. To reference our past in any way. I was here to do a job.

Take him home.

"Probably wise."

He stepped past me, deeper into his office. I didn't turn, gathering myself, so I heard rather than saw him sit in a squealing chair and open a drawer, and I knew without turning that he'd be taking out the bottle of akvavit.

The champagne and the whiskey—they were for show. That terrible vodka he hawked from every billboard and magazine ad, totally for show.

The akvavit was for him.

I turned and saw him pour clear liquid into two shot glasses.

He lifted one toward me but I didn't take it.

"Really?" he asked. "It's one of Alec's best batches."

Of course he kept in touch with Alec.

"I'm here on official business," I said. "Not to drink Alec's burnwine."

"You stayed at the palace." It wasn't a question. He knew I'd stayed. He sat back in his chair, the old springs squeaking at the effort. I couldn't place his careful tone. He'd lost the sneer and sounded, if possible, hopeful.

"You left. Someone had to stay and make sure your father and his brother didn't sell Vasgar to the devils."

His brow furrowed. "The council members we worked with? Vera? John?"

"There was a massive turnover about a year and a half ago, your Uncle's doing. But Vera stayed. John was replaced by someone your uncle backed."

He swore under his breath and it was a relief to see he still cared. After three years and from the bottom of this New York City club—he still cared.

"And so, you stayed to fight the good fight?" he asked, leaning back in his chair, his shirt shifting to reveal the snarling mouth of the wolf on his chest.

"I've kept your uncle from the throne and I've been running the country in your father's illness. I'm all but queen."

"But not queen."

"The council members would not hear my petition."

He gaped at me. "You petitioned council?"

"They know I've been running the country. They know I'm more than capable. I am a member of the royal family. Your father made me princess."

The decision of the council still burned. The misogyny and sexism of our government was a rock I could not roll aside on my own. No matter how hard I fought. My mother —she could have helped, but she was working far too hard on her role as grieving widow.

"So they didn't let you speak, and instead sent you to come fetch me, the black sheep prince. Oh, this must be a humbling moment for you."

I said nothing, because the pride lodged in my throat would not allow it.

"I meant what I told you years ago. You are not meant for the throne of Vasgar."

I'd been expecting it in some way. For him to throw that moment in my face like an animal kicking up dust.

I could feel my cheeks blushing. My neck. And he noticed, his eyes narrowing, which only made me blush harder. Underneath my coat I felt every inch of my body, all my skin.

"They didn't send me," I said. "I've come on my own. The council wants your uncle."

I watched Gunnar, cruelty on his face, pour another shot of akvavit and hold it out to me in his elegant fingers. "Nothing goes better with pride than Alec's burnwine. Go on."

"I am a far better ruler than you will be," I said and took the shot because I felt my walls crumbling. It burned down my throat, cleared away the memories. Focused my intentions.

"Of that," he said with a sigh, "there has never been any

doubt. But why are you here for me when the council didn't send you?"

"Because if you don't come back, the throne will go to your uncle. And I have worked too hard to see that happen."

Gunnar knew that, of course. His uncle was second in line. The world was so unfair.

But he sharpened. That lazy indolence he'd perfected to hide the fact that he had a thinking brain and a beating heart vanished for the moment and it was him there. The man I'd loved.

"And my uncle?"

"As long as your dad was alive we could keep him at arm's length." I didn't go into what that had entailed. What it had cost me. Or what I'd gained.

"And now? He's making an advance toward the throne?"

"You're not there to stop it," I said.

"How bad is it?"

"He has made no secret of his plans to sell the oil drilling rights in Brinmark Sound," I said.

"But you had that foreign investment. You managed to keep the rights—"

"How do you know that?"

"I read newspapers, Brenna. I might have left that doesn't mean I stopped caring. I was with you, those last few months—"

I coughed, interrupting him. Unable to discuss those last few months and the work we'd done.

"Your uncle isn't satisfied with the slow progress allowed by the investment. He wants more and he's already brought the Russian president in for meetings. Gazprom has bought a building in the capital."

"Jesus," he said, and I was so gratified to see his shock.

That's right, asshole, that's what you allowed to happen when you left.

That wasn't totally fair to Gunnar, but I wasn't interested in being fair.

"All that work three years ago, those things you started. I've kept them going," I said. "But if you don't come back, it's all over. I can't fight your uncle and council."

And the truth was, I had a million reasons to hate Gunnar. The way he'd treated me, the way he'd abandoned me. His casual cruelty. His vanity and ego. All of them fuel to the fire of my anger and hurt and resentment.

But he poured himself one more shot, drained it and then stood. Tall and strong and more than enough to defeat his uncle. Gunnar might have hated his father—and with good reason—but he loved his country.

"I assume you have a jet waiting?"

"At JFK," I said. "A car is out front."

He took a deep breath and then smiled, like this was all just a lark. "Then let's go make me king."

From a hook behind him he grabbed a long black cashmere overcoat and swung it around his shoulders, already looking so much like a king it made my heart pinch in my chest.

9

T HEN
Vasgar
Brenna

I CAME BACK AT CHRISTMAS, braving an epic snowstorm and a terrible flight because my mother begged me. It had been too long, she'd said. Which was something she never said. Missing me wasn't something she'd seemed capable of. Until now. Though my suspicion was that the honeymoon was over and she felt very far away from everything that was familiar to her.

And I was the one familiar thing she could bring back to the palace.

I was nervous. Not just because of the flight. Or returning to the castle, which had never stopped being a kind of enemy territory. I was nervous seeing Gunnar again.

As a friend.

We'd texted while I was at school. A surprising amount,

really. It started with him sending a picture of Alec, sleeping on the couch in Gunnar's room.

I think you forgot this, he'd written.

It escalated from there. Pictures of his life and of mine. Funny things we'd seen. Questions about our parents.

My mother seems lonely, I wrote to him.

Everyone here is lonely, he'd written back.

I sent him articles about the oil industry in Aberdeen.

He sent me articles on palace gossip.

But then there'd been three months of questions about Aberdeen's oil industry.

The driver dropped me at the side entrance of the palace. The only entrance with a cover, so the snow wasn't very deep. The wind was vicious and the guards could barely wrestle the doors open enough for me to stagger inside.

Which I did, bringing the cold and some snow with me. The silence of the hall was thick as cotton after the wind-whipped noise of the outside world. I leaned back against the door, catching my breath, my glasses fogging up over the seven hundred feet of red scarf I was wearing.

"Welcome home, Princess." Oh, god, it was Gunnar.

That sardonic dark curl to his voice was unmistakable and my body, despite the chill, went hot. I couldn't see him, thanks to the scarf and the foggy glasses. But I could feel him like a heat source in front of me.

"Hello Gunnar." I picked myself up off the door as I heard him walking closer.

"Need some help?" he asked, his voice full of banked laughter. Like a fire ready to blaze into being. It had gotten so I read his texts and heard that buried humor. That voice was in my head.

"I don't know if you can find me in all this."

"I can probably manage."

He took one edge of the long red scarf and began to unwind it. Slowly revealing my face. My glasses bobbled on my nose and I grabbed them. I still couldn't see him, he was a blurry dark blob smiling at me.

"There you are," he said.

I put my glasses back on, the fog reduced to the edges of the lenses so I could see him clearly.

I had tried over the last few months to tell myself that he was not nearly as handsome as I remembered. It had been the shock of him—a royal prince and everything. And the romance of the summer wedding. There was simply no way he'd looked as good as I remembered. Or was as charismatic.

Well, guess what? He was. The jerk.

That half curl to his lip, the sparkle in his eye that I knew, I knew down to my bones, was for me. He was happy to see me. As happy to see me as I was to see him.

"Where...ah...where are our parents?" I asked. All this happiness felt dangerous. Like this moment—this just-friends moment—might break under the weight of all this happiness and maybe become something...else. Something it wasn't supposed to be.

"They're waiting for you in the living room."

"Why are you here?"

"Because I knew this was the only entrance that was protected and so it was most likely they'd bring you here."

"And you wanted—"

"To see you, Brenna." He pushed my messy hair back behind my ear, his touch sending shock waves all across my skin. Down through my bones. "I just wanted to see you."

Yeah. This didn't feel like just friends.

. . .

EIGHT MONTHS Later
 Gunnar

BRENNA HAD STAYED in the UK for the summer.

Working for The McDonald Group, which handled oil logistics and management for the government of Scotland. She was getting all the answers to all the questions we'd had from the inside. And she wanted to organize a meeting between me and Donal McDonald.

After Christmas, she hadn't come back once. And I didn't blame her. Shit was awful at the palace.

So I told her to book the meeting and I went to her. In Aberdeen. In August.

Yeah. Sure. We'd figure out some oil rights stuff. But mostly—I'd decided—we were going to fuck each other's brains out.

This just-friends stuff wasn't working. It was a stupid idea the day we came up with it on the boat. It was stupid at Christmas. It was stupid every time we pretended to just be friends when we texted twenty million times a day.

We weren't fucking friends.

So I told my father and my uncle and the entire country that I was going to Ibiza for a week and no one batted an eye. I left the family jet in London and booked an economy ticket (gasp!) to Aberdeen. And a room at The Chester.

The sky in Aberdeen was low and gray, the kind of sky that made you hunch your shoulders against it. Like you needed to do your part to carry the load. But I'd been buoyed the whole flight by a certain inevitability about this week. How right it felt. If there was fallout we'd handle it later. Handling fallout was kind of my one great talent.

I told her she didn't need to pick me up. That I would

make my way to The Chester and meet her downtown. But I recognized her right away, waiting near the taxi stand. A long row of cars with anxious loved ones was picking up other arrivals.

She wore a red dress, the skirt of which was tugged and lifted by a cold breeze. I imagined that dress on the floor of my room in The Chester and smiled.

"Hello, Gunnar," she said once I was close.

"I told you, you didn't need to come."

"I told you, I wanted to." She smiled at me with her whole face. Her whole body. And she probably thought that smile was what made us friends. The joy we seemed to share in seeing each other. And maybe she felt that way about other men and maybe I would have to murder them.

We hugged, managing to elbow awkwardness out of the way for the moment.

"It's good to see you," she said somewhere in the vicinity of my neck, and her breath on my skin and the feel of her body against mine sent blood thumping through my veins.

"Brenna," I said, ready to kiss her. Needing to kiss her.

"Oi!" a man yelled. "Brenna, we got to get a move on."

Brenna pulled back and ducked down to smile at the man in the gray sedan idling at the curb. "Sorry, Daniel. Thanks. Pop the boot, yeah?"

"Daniel?" I asked.

Brenna grabbed my bag like she was going to carry it and I put my hand on hers. But she didn't look at me and that buoyant sense of inevitability took a disastrous hit. And I couldn't believe it but I was suddenly jealous of a man who would sit in a car and let a woman handle another man's baggage.

"Nice of your friend to give us a ride," I said.

"Daniel's my boyfriend."

. . .

ONE YEAR Later
  Gunnar

IT WAS my second secret meeting in the library. And it was going about as well as the first. Which was to say...terribly.

Embarrassingly, really.

The meeting included Alec, Ingrid, and the new council members, John Garfield and Vera Wilkinson who'd gone from mayor of Brinmark Sound to council member when Ann Jorgenson retired. And even though she agreed with what I was trying to do, Vera still didn't like me.

I wished Brenna were here.

She would be amazing at this.

I tried to resist the urge to check my watch for possibly the hundredth time in the last hour but Brenna was due to arrive in... Damn it, I checked my watch.

Twenty minutes.

"Are we boring you, Gunnar?" Vera asked.

"You called this meeting," John said. He leaned back and his chair squeaked in protest. John Garfield came from the center of South Island, where it seemed all the men were built on a slightly larger scale. "Hate to think we're keeping you from something you'd rather do."

"No, of course not," I said. "I'm trying to enlist your help in convincing other council members to our side in this oil drilling issue."

"Our side," Vera said with a sniff. "You have a long way to go, Gunnar if you're trying to convince my constituents that you are on *our* side."

Vera was cruel and gave no points for trying.

Since the council voted to keep the oil rights and get foreign investment, my father and my uncle had thrown up thousands of road blocks to keep that investment from coming in.

So, we were still cash poor. But the rights were ours.

Though there had been turn over in the council and my uncle and father were working for a new vote on the sale of the oil rights all while creating complete chaos in the country, dividing support between investment and sale.

And now the fisheries were in trouble.

"Well, it's my side that's kept the oil rights in our hands and not in the Russians'." My side had Brenna and her contacts and hard work at The MacDonald Group. "So you're stuck with me. With the turnover on the council, we lost some allies. We need new ones. Which is why we're here."

"Your father and uncle have done nothing but create problems for us since we voted down the sale of the oil rights," John said.

"I know," I said. "They've blocked the money from investors and slowed down the process more than any of us anticipated."

"So what are we going to do?" John asked.

"Get creative."

"Agatha Viisk from South Island, I believe, is in agreement," Vera said. "I can talk to her."

"We can talk until we turn blue," said John. "And it won't change the fact that we need money, Gunnar. The investment hasn't happened yet and now our fisheries are dying. In the last year, the council has brought five very acceptable and very rich women to your attention. All of whom would gladly sit on the throne when you become king."

"The last one," said Alec. My old friend was now a

trusted advisor, though I'd cheerfully stab him in the eye at the moment. "The heiress from the States. She was beautiful, too."

She'd been as thin and as cold as an icicle.

And I totally understood that was my fate. I accepted it... I just wanted a little more time.

One more summer. This summer. Brenna was home for a few months, for some mysterious reason no one was telling me but I thought had to do with her mother's unhappiness.

And I really hoped it didn't have anything to do with Daniel.

One summer. And then I'd do my part and consider the American Heiress.

"It's not the Middle Ages," Vera said, her support in this arena a never-ending surprise. "The boy should marry who he wants."

"The 'boy' is twenty-seven years old, and in parts of our kingdom it feels like the Middle Ages," John said, and I was ashamed he was right.

The seal of the library door cracked and someone walked into the room. Everyone at the table looked at each other and began to gather up their things. Tucked away as we were, we couldn't see the door and everyone was paranoid it would be my father or uncle or any of their minions.

I could tell them not to worry. Even without looking I knew it was Brenna. A few minutes early. Making her way from the door to the back corner she loved best.

I didn't have to see her to know.

There was her smell—juniper and lavender. And an electrical current in the air. My body came awake as if from a long sleep.

Itching and twitchy with my awareness of her.

"I'll consider wives in a few months," I said as everyone stood up. "And I understand patience is difficult. We can save our fisheries, I'm sure of it. And they might just save us."

"I think you're crazy, boy," John said. "Fishing ain't gonna save this country. But I'm willing to give you a few more months of freedom before marrying you off to the highest bidder."

Alec laughed but swallowed it when I glared at him.

I shut the door behind everyone and then turned, fighting my smile.

Brenna.

She was right where I thought she'd be, folded up in one of the leather chairs at the wide oak table that had been carved by the Vikings that settled on this island.

Her cheeky grin had an effect on me I could not pin down. The whole of her had an effect on me I couldn't pin down and I didn't try. There were no more boxes for this woman and how I felt about her.

What amazed me about her, though, was she could sit there and seem both completely foreign and completely familiar at the same time.

Same long blond hair, piercing blue eyes, her gaze stabbing at me through her glasses. A book in her hands.

A force of nature I could not predict or control.

Our last summer, I thought with a pang that felt like regret and relief all at once.

"Hello, Brenna," I said, leaning against the table. "Sorry I couldn't meet you in the throne room."

"It's all right. I figured your meeting ran long. How is the cloak and dagger business going?" she said, cutting right to the chase. Which, really, was the thing she did. And she was the only one who did it in this palace. She saw right to the heart of the matter and then ran directly at it.

I sighed and ran my hands over my face. I was exhausted. Herding cats and trying to influence things from the shadows behind my father was not as easy as I'd thought it would be.

What had made me think I could do this?

"Gunnar?" She stood up, stepping closer to me. Her voice was steeped in sympathy and worry, and I wanted more than I could say to pull her into my arms. Rest my chin against her head and let her support me for a few seconds.

But that would cross the lines we'd put between us. The just-friends agreement and Daniel. The literal miles and miles between us—all of the walls created to stop us from what we wanted to do.

We texted for hours every week. But we never touched. And that reverse intimacy threw me off.

She had grown into her Viking princess looks while she'd been at school and I could barely keep my eyes off her. She owned her height, wearing tall boots that made her even taller. And tight jeans that flaunted her legs and the round curve of her ass.

It caused problems every time we were together. Problems I worked hard to hide. But I was so damn tired. And so damn alone here in the shadows. How was I supposed to marry the heiress when Brenna and her legs were out there in the world?

So when she came toward me with all her concern and friendship and those fucking legs of hers—I stepped back.

Which of course made her stop. She pressed her hand to her stomach, fiddling with the bottom edge of her shirt.

Our weird intimacy made it easy to hurt each other, too.

We were all prickles and spikes. And I didn't know how to stop it.

"I'm fine," I said with a smile that tried to bridge the cavern we kept between us. "But the clock is ticking. Dad's had another heart attack. And my uncle, the greedy fucker, is trying to grab power through this oil thing."

"And you're going to stop him?"

"I'm heir to the throne of Vasgar, Brenna. If I don't stop him, who will? If I don't lead this country out of the dark days my dad put us in, who will? My uncle would have us annexed to Russia in three years."

She was silent for so long I looked up and caught her staring at me, her bottom lip between her teeth.

Fuck, I wanted to suck on that lip. Every time we saw each other she was different. Not just more beautiful, which she was, brilliantly so. Almost painfully so. But she was more and more herself. Sharper, somehow. Clearer.

And now, standing in front of me, she was the epitome of the difference between attractive, which she'd always been, and magnetic.

She was absolutely magnetic.

I'd never seen this coming. This slow and steady evolution of her.

And my growing inability to resist her.

"Look at you," she said with a bright smile.

No. No. Honey, look at you.

"I guess someone wore off on me." We looked at each other, that connection simmering between us with absolutely nowhere to go before she turned away toward the stained glass windows. Squares of blue light shone down on her face.

Are you still with Daniel? Tell me you're not with Daniel.

"I want to help," she said. "With the council. With the vote. With...everything you're doing."

"Help? What about your life in Scotland?" *Daniel.*

"I've got a few months until I go to New York."

"New York?" I said. *A few months?* "Brenna, enough with the secrets. What's going on? Why are you home?"

"I got the job at the UN. Starting in the New Year."

"The UN?"

She nodded.

A slow smile spread across my face.

"Brenna—"

"Stop."

"No! That's amazing! How long have you known?"

"Awhile."

"Why didn't you tell me?"

"I don't know." She glanced at me and then away. Pleased and nervous. So unbearably Brenna. "I wanted to tell you in person."

"My god, Brenna. Congratulations," I said and stepped toward her. The lines between us buzzed their warning, insisting that we keep our distance, threatening terrible things if we ignored those warnings.

But this was huge, the beginning of all her dreams, and I pulled her into my arms.

She fit there, against my chest, under my chin, just like I suspected she would. We each inhaled, our stomachs touched, her breath feathered over my neck. The ends of her long hair stroked over my fingers and I couldn't resist tangling them in those strands.

Her hands spread wide over my back like she was trying to feel as much of me as she could. Like with her hands she could memorize me. I knew she was doing it because I was doing it, too.

We had this one moment. One moment and we both took advantage of it. Soaking the sensation of the other in through our skins like rain-starved earth.

I breathed in the smell of her, trapping it in my lungs. In my head.

She laughed, a strange little chuckle, and I felt it against my chest.

I held her as long as I could. Until the never-ending hum between us got my dick hard. Until it would be impossible to hide how much I wanted her. Then I held her at arm's length for a second, letting her go in pieces.

"So proud of you, Brenna."

"Thank you, Gunnar."

She stepped back with a cocky little smile that went right to my blood. She was entirely a creature of contradiction—confidence and vulnerability in equal turns.

"But, come on, sit down, tell me your plans," she said.

She's not for you, I told myself. *She's not for Vasgar. She is meant for big things. Do not get used to her being around.*

The smart thing to do would be to leave. Give us some much-needed space. But I didn't. I sat down.

WITHIN A WEEK we were knee-deep in palace intrigue. We were a team. Alec and Ingrid joined us and the library was our office. So far, no other council members appeared to be joining our side. Or if they were, they weren't telling me about it.

"The problem," Ingrid said, "is that no one thinks you're going to lead."

I sat back down in what had become my seat at the head of the Viking table. Which at this point was covered with laptops and dirty dishes from the meal we'd eaten while working. The many meals.

My uncle was making a play to take the council by bribery and influence. It was an awkward fight between us in the shadows. Painfully political when what I wanted to do was punch my uncle in the face.

"She's right," Alec agreed. "Your reputation precedes you."

"You need a new reputation," Brenna said. Her blond hair was pulled up into a bun on the top of her head. It was messy and wild with a pencil stuck right through it. She wore her glasses because her contacts bothered her late at night and these glasses had clear frames. Very funky. Very different from what she usually wore and I found myself a little obsessed with them.

Wondering what had made her change her style.

Fucking Daniel.

"He needs Brenna's reputation." Ingrid laughed like it was a joke, but Brenna and I turned wide eyes to each other.

"I'm attending a reading tomorrow night," she said, flipping through her calendar. "Poetry followed by a discussion led by the artist."

"I'll accompany you."

"And two days after that I'm speaking at a luncheon for high school leadership students."

"Perfect," I said.

"Perhaps you should do the speaking," she said, already making notes on her phone. "I could tweak my speech for you."

"No," I said, uncomfortable with how quickly she would hand me that when it was her work and decency they wanted at that luncheon. "I don't think—"

"Just a few words," Ingrid agreed. "Perhaps you could introduce her."

"Great idea," Alec said. "There's also a business association conference next week that I'm going to. I could talk to Ronin and get Gunnar on the program. Same sort of thing —he could introduce Ronin or something."

The three of them kept talking, discussing speech writing and the possibility of hiring an old friend of Ingrid's who had been working in London for a while, writing speeches for the mayor.

"She'd come back?" Alec asked.

"To work for her own country?" Ingrid said like it was a done deal.

"To work for me, the wastrel prince?" I asked, because we needed to get real here for a second.

"Good point," Ingrid said. "But...I can convince her."

"We can convince everyone," Brenna said, looking right at me. "People love a good redemption story. And we can give them that."

"You're going to redeem me?" I asked her, smiling at how unlikely that was.

"You don't think I can?" she asked.

"I think you can do just about anything you want," I said. Aware in an offhand way of Ingrid and Alec sharing a knowing look.

"It's the wedding waltz all over again," Alec said.

"Hey!" Ingrid was sharp and loud, and Brenna and I broke eye contact to find her frowning at us. "You want to be king?" Ingrid asked. "You want to change your reputation? You want to convince everyone you are ready to lead?"

I nodded.

"Then you two are friends only."

"That's all we've ever been," I said. Ingrid pointed at Brenna, who was blushing red hot.

Her skin flushed so fast I was surprised the papers around her didn't catch on fire. That kiss in Brinmark Sound was right there on her face.

"No problem," Brenna said and looked away.

But even then, we both knew it was going to be a huge problem.

CHAPTER 10

THEN
  Brenna

Just friends.

Such an innocuous thing. Of course we were just friends. Family of a kind. Nothing more. It was and always had been painfully obvious that we were nothing more. Could never be anything more. Despite that kiss.

It was just a kiss. A stupid...kiss. A stupid kiss I'd replayed a million times in my head. A stupid kiss that crept into my brain when I was alone with my fingers between my legs.

It meant nothing to him; I knew that. The same way I knew it meant way too much to me.

I'd broken up with Daniel before I came home. Daniel, who I'd been with for the better part of a year. Daniel, who on paper was perfect for me.

But what felt right out there in the world never felt right in Vasgar.

Only Gunnar felt right in Vasgar.

Only Gunnar.

We were walking to the poetry reading by the Nobel Prize winner from Sweden. A feminist whose daughter had died of an overdose on the streets of New York. It was going to be a powerful night and the kind of place no one would expect Gunnar to show up.

The Facebook and Instagram posts from the people in the hall were going to do half our work for us.

The summer night was warm and the streets of Vernis, the capital city, were full of families and couples. The ice cream shops were doing a good business and I was working so hard at making sure I didn't accidentally touch Gunnar that I kept tripping off the curb.

"Brenna, you all right?" Gunnar asked, taking my elbow to pull me back up onto the sidewalk.

"Fine." His fingers on my skin caused an excitement so acute it almost felt like dread.

"I like your glasses," he said. "They're new."

When he said things like that, things that indicated he'd noticed me and small things about me, I didn't know what to do. Or how to act. I pushed the glasses up higher on my nose and thanked him.

"Not your usual style," he said.

"What is my usual style?" I asked, laughing, because I didn't even know what my usual style was.

"I'm just saying they're funky."

"A friend helped me pick them out," I said, nervous for no real reason. "He's pretty funky."

"Daniel?" he asked, and I stopped and stared at him. Happy families with ice cream cones walked around us like we were stones in a river. And I wanted to remind myself of a dozen things. That we were just friends. That I had imagined his disappointment at the Aberdeen airport. That he did not actually feel what I wanted him to feel.

I'd seen the pictures of him with the American heiress and they had been a pinprick right to the center of my heart. Not a fatal wound but a deeply uncomfortable one.

They'd gone out to dinner in Helsinki. A casual thing. But I knew nothing about it was casual.

We stared at each other, still as rocks oblivious to the river rushing by.

How could he care about Daniel when he had the heiress? Why did I care about Daniel when he had the heiress?

But none of that mattered. Not really. Because this summer it was Vasgar. And it was Gunnar.

"We broke up," I said.

"I'm sorry," he said, but he wasn't.

He took my elbow and put us back into motion toward the theater where the poetry reading was being held. We walked that way for a moment, arm in arm, the tender skin inside our elbows touching. But then people started to notice us...well, Gunnar. And I moved my arm away and shifted sideways until there was more space between us, because the story had to be Gunnar and not us.

Because gossip about us would derail everything we were working for.

And we weren't a story. We were a summer. That was all.

No one was as surprised as me that Gunnar loved the poetry reading.

Except maybe Gunnar.

"Did you read her short story in the *New Yorker*?" he asked me a few days later as we were heading to the High School Leadership Conference.

"Oh, my god, you're still obsessed?"

"Obsessed?" He shot me a look. "Well, maybe...but seriously, check out that story. It will break your heart. I'll email it to you."

He fiddled around with his phone and then I heard the bing of my own in my purse. We were in the back of the limo and only had about five more minutes until we were at the high school where the conference was being held. "Read it and your heart will never be the same."

Jesus. Come on. It was completely unfair that Gunnar looked the way he did. Now he was talking about poetry and its effect on his heart? Who could resist this guy?

Me. I could. But I didn't want to...

"Really, Gunnar. Can we focus on the speech for today?"

He waved his hand. "I've got the speech for today. Don't sweat it."

I wasn't, really, because if there was one aspect of this redemption that was flawless it was Gunnar in front of a crowd. He was a natural showman. Charming and sincere. Earnest, even. He'd killed it at the Vasgar Business Association with Alec.

And people were really starting to notice.

"Deiter from the *Times* has asked for an interview," I said.

"Not yet."

I glanced up from my phone. "What do you mean, not yet?"

"I mean we've been to three functions. I've given one speech. Let's do some more work before we take a lap around the newspapers."

I blinked at him.

"What?" he asked.

"You're so...good at this."

"Brenna," he said with a smile that was indulgent and endearing all at the same time. "I've been a prince my whole life. Politics, whether I like or not, is a game I am very good at. I've just never played politics with real issues before."

I tilted my head and looked at him. So handsome, so dapper in the black suit with the white dress shirt underneath it. He managed to be informal and formal at the same time. Every high school girl in that gymnasium was going to lose her mind for him.

"What changed?" I asked.

"What do you mean?"

"Why do you care now?"

That indulgent smile slid right off his face just as the car slowed down in front of the school. We came to a stop and Gunnar's bodyguard got out of the front seat and opened our door. I could hear the crowd outside the high school, screaming Gunnar's name. There were bright pops of flash photography but Gunnar didn't turn. Or wave.

He simply sat and looked at me, his handsome face careful and still.

"Do you really not know?" he asked.

I'd forgotten what I asked. What were we talking about?

"You," he said. "I care because of you."

And then he turned, arm lifted, smile wide, and stepped from the car, pausing to help me out.

"Go," I said, rattled and blushing. Removing myself from his touch as fast as I could. "Go ahead. Shake hands. Answer questions."

He did as I told him, stepping to the lineup of people who'd been waiting for a glimpse of him. Heart in my throat, I watched him. I watched him be the kind of leader his people needed. The kind of leader I'd always hoped he'd be. Even before I knew him.

CHAPTER 11

T HEN
Gunnar

DAD CAME DOWN TO BREAKFAST. I was so surprised I actually got to my feet to help him into his chair. God, he'd aged. He was still a young man, but he looked eighty. The last heart attack had drained him and he wasn't coming back from it like he had the first one. He was one tone of gray, from his hair to his face to his hands, which shook around his teacup.

"Dad," I said settling back into my seat and stacking up the papers I'd been looking at. "It's good to see you up."

"Really," he said, not a question but a statement with a message I didn't fully understand.

"Of course," I said. "Where is Annika?"

"Who knows?" He nudged his plate forward. "Get me some of the sausage, would you?"

"You sure you should be having sausage?"

"Do you honestly think it matters?" he asked, blinking his watery eyes at me.

I gaped, stunned by this morose and defeatist version of my father.

The king.

But like the good son I'd never particularly been, I stood up and got him two of the venison sausages. But I also picked up a tomato and some of the blueberries that were ripe this time of year.

"You've been busy," Dad said as I sat back down. "Poetry readings and the like." He shoved the newspaper on the table over toward me. There was a picture on the front page of me at the high school leadership event. I was standing on the steps of the school, waving over my shoulder at the crowd standing there.

Brenna stood next to me, focused on her phone.

I shrugged, pretending I didn't know what he was getting at. "You've been after me to be more involved in life outside of bars and parties."

His laughter turned into a wheezing cough.

"Father—"

"Making Brenna into your assistant doesn't look good."

"She's not my assistant," I said.

"Looks like your assistant." He tapped the photograph and I uncomfortably had to admit in that picture she looked...assistant-like. "But that's neither here or there. I need you to go to Helsinki this weekend. A state function. A dinner and a tour of the fisheries there."

"Excellent. Brenna was just telling me about their innovative—"

"I need you to hear me," he said and grabbed my hand with his own. His palm was dry and rough, like a husk. It was so startling, I looked down to see if it was actually his skin touching my skin. I couldn't remember the last time my father had held my hand in a grip that wasn't cruel. "You will be king someday."

"I know. And I'm trying to earn the title—"

He waved my words away like they meant nothing. "You've already earned it. You were born to me. You're my son. The way I was my father's. Down the line for hundreds of years."

I remembered thinking that way. How entitled I'd felt to the crown and to the position. To my country's loyalty and all that entailed. And then Brenna came along and changed everything. Over the last year I'd wanted to earn her loyalty and, in a broader sense, the country's. I wanted her respect.

The last few weeks with her, traveling back and forth to these small conferences and poetry readings, museums and galleries, it felt as if I were seeing my country for the first time. And as the photographers descended and the social media posts were less about me in a bar and more about me talking to my fellow citizens, it felt as if I was seeing myself for the first time.

The man I could be. The man my country needed me to be.

These last few weeks had been some of the best of my life.

And Brenna had everything to do with that.

Assistant, my ass.

"And," he said, his eyes narrowing until I felt like he was slicing right through me. "You will be forgiven a lot. The drinking and the partying. The inappropriate women. The gossip about threesomes in hotel rooms. They can call you a wastrel and you will still be king."

"That's what I'm trying to say, Father. I don't want the country to call me that. I want to be a good king."

"They will love you when you marry the heiress."

"That's a long way off." I'd become so good at not thinking about it that I'd almost convinced myself it wouldn't happen. That, through pure force of will, I could make it not happen.

"You need to stay away from Brenna."

I sat back, my father's hand falling away. "There's nothing happening between me and Brenna."

"That is undoubtedly bullshit," he said.

"I'm not lying."

"All you do is lie. You're my son, Gunnar. No one knows your dark, disappointing heart like I do."

I stood up, this conversation so over. So completely over. I'd thought he'd lost the power to hurt me with his dislike. It was disappointing to realize I was wrong.

"You are all but engaged to the heiress."

"No one has said one word about engagement. I had dinner with her!" One awful formal, stilted dinner with a very rich woman who, like the queen now, was only interested in wearing the crown.

"One whiff of something between you and Brenna and I'll banish her, Gunnar," he said. My feet stopped. My heart. Everything. Stopped. Banished? These were modern times. That was an old law that was turning to dust in the history books. "I'll send her so far away, it will be like she was never here."

"You don't think her mother will have something to say about that?" I asked, laughing a little at his ridiculousness.

"Annika wanted to be queen," he said with a shrug that explained every shallow inch of their relationship. God, how sad that Brenna had been right the night of their wedding. How awful that I seemed doomed to repeat it.

"Why wouldn't you banish me?"

"Don't tempt me, Gunnar."

"You're not that powerful," I said.

"You have no idea of my power. I've done more for lesser crimes. Don't test me on this, Gunnar. She's turned into a passable woman who will no doubt marry some needle-dicked intellectual and she'll—"

"Stop, Father. Stop."

"She's not for you."

I stared down at my father, so disgusted by him and his blood that ran in my veins. "She's not for any of us," I said and left the breakfast table and my father behind.

CHAPTER 12

T HEN
Brenna

"YOU'RE IN A MOOD," I said from the banquette across from Gunnar. We were in the jet heading to Helsinki and I was reading the reports of Sweden's innovations in their fisheries. Specifically, the innovation in selectivity through on-net or alternative technologies.

I didn't understand a word of it. But I figured someone needed to read it by tomorrow's tour of the fisheries. And it looked like that person would not be Gunnar.

"I'm in a great mood," he said, lifting his drink toward me in a sardonic toast.

"You're going to be drunk before we even get to the dinner." I looked down at the papers I was trying to read but all my concentration was wrapped up in Gunnar and this strange mood.

He'd always been magnetic to me. Someone I had to

work to keep at arm's length. It was easier when I was in Scotland, texting him from my bed at night. I'd even managed to convince myself that the attraction I'd felt had only been a kind of adrenaline-fueled walk on the wild side.

He was not the man for me.

But still I broke up with Daniel and decided not to go back to Edinburgh before the UN job. I came home for him. To be with him in whatever way I could.

But now, after the last few weeks...I had to admit I was in trouble. Gunnar had changed and maybe I was changing, too. Maybe the world we were living in was changing. And keeping myself to myself was getting harder and harder to do.

But something had happened yesterday or today and it seemed like he'd slipped back into his old clothes. Biting and smiling all at once. Uninterested and impossibly interesting at the same time.

"Unfortunately not." He looked out the window at the darkness of the North Sea beneath us. Frigid and distant. God, I thought, how did we get back here?

"What happened, Gunnar?" I asked. "What's changed? A few days ago—"

"My father called you my assistant."

I jerked back, wounded a little but not surprised. "Your dad is an ass."

"But how long until he mentions that to someone else, who mentions it to Deiter who puts it on the front page? And then the entire country—"

"I don't care." Which wasn't entirely true.

"I do." His gray eyes burned when he looked at me. "My father is a caveman and my uncle is worse, and they'll poison everyone against you if it suits them."

I pushed aside the papers and left my banquette to sit

beside him on his. He jolted, as if I'd sat myself in his lap. "Your father is an old man who not only wasted his opportunity to be a better man but will ruin your efforts to do the same. Don't let him get to you."

He looked at me, unreadable and unknowable. As distant as that sea. And I didn't look away, feeling somehow like I needed to drill those words and my belief in him into his brain myself.

"Why do you think I'm any different?" he asked me.

"From your father?" I laughed. "Because I've seen you. Because I know you."

He touched my face with the tips of his fingers and I gasped. I couldn't stop myself. This wasn't allowed.

No touching. Not ever.

And I'd worked hard to forget the electric reality of his skin against mine.

"You're leaving," he said and licked his lips as if he, too, had been startled into feeling something by the contact of our skin. "The UN job."

I wasn't sure what he was getting at. Was he worried I was going to work to get him into power and then abandon him? "Vasgar will always be my home."

"But you won't live here. Because you're going to be amazing," he said. "Far away from Vasgar."

That had been the plan—the North Star I steered my entire life by. But right now, with this new Gunnar, that plan no longer seemed so important. The last few weeks we'd settled into something that felt like a partnership. But I couldn't tell him that. He would fight me on it and Gunnar rarely fought fair.

"You're going to be amazing for Vasgar," I told him. He watched me for a long moment, then he lifted his fingertips from my skin, put down the drink, and asked for the fisheries summary.

I felt that touch for hours afterward.

THEN

Gunnar

WHEN I WAS A KID, Alec dared me to jump off the cliffs at Lake Fasso. Lake Fasso was our deepest lake and maybe our coldest. It was in August, which meant the lake had been thawed for a week and would be thawed for perhaps another week before the weather changed and its black water iced over again.

Never able to resist a dare, I climbed up the cliffs, cutting my hands on granite and slipping on green lichen until I found an outcropping I could get both feet on and I looked down and thought, *I'm only nervous because I don't know how deep or cold it actually is. Once I know, I won't be nervous.*

And I jumped. And it was so cold, it hurt. My body went into shock and I drifted down and down and down into its terrible depths.

Alec jumped in and grabbed me, pulling us both back to shore where we shivered in the sunlight.

Touching Brenna was like that. I'd been so blindly confident before stroking the smooth skin of her cheek with my fingers. I was sure my memories of how soft she was were exaggerated. By time. By the fact that I *couldn't* touch her.

Surely a touch wouldn't be trouble.

But now, at this damn dinner, I was still shaking off the sensation of her skin. I was still marvelling at her beauty and my stupidity.

I still wanted her. The desire I'd felt for her a year ago was a shadow compared to this.

Across the room she was talking to a group of fishery experts. I guessed that because everyone seemed to be fishery experts at this event. The king was a fisheries expert.

I should be, too.

"I'm sorry to hear about your father's health," the king, sitting beside me, said. He was young for a king, forty-three. Which meant he would be on the throne for a long time. And while the title was mostly an honorific, the king of Sweden got shit done.

"Thank you," I said. "And I pass on his greetings and good wishes to you and the royal family."

He smiled slightly, a handsome man with silver-blond hair. He was taller than I was, which was saying something.

"Can I give you a bit of advice, one son to another?"

"Of course."

"Care more for your people than your crown. It was a lesson my father didn't teach me and I had to learn the hard way."

"That's excellent advice," I said, distracted by Brenna laughing at the far end of the room. Some scientist over there was a real comedian and she was flushed and smiling.

Which is how it should be. I want her to be happy. And I want her far away from Vasgar. And me.

The role my father and uncle would force her into. The limits they would impose on her abilities because she was a threat to their old-white-man sense of power.

No. Impossible.

She had to go her way and I would go mine. And my way was the future of Vasgar.

I turned to the king. "To that end, Your Majesty, I would like to discuss your fisheries."

. . .

THE PARTY WAS OVER and I walked Brenna down the long silent hallways to our rooms in the royal palace. This end of the building was hushed and quiet.

"Remember how I used to get lost in the palace?" Brenna asked. Her hair was slipping out of her topknot and trailing down her back, white gold and silky.

It burned in my fingertips, the memory of exactly how silky her hair was.

I tucked my hands into my pockets so I wouldn't reach out and touch it.

"I do," I said, smiling.

"I spent hours lost in that damn castle," she said.

So have I.

"You seemed to be having fun tonight," I said, and she looked up at me with wide, laughing eyes.

"Sven, the head scientist on the fisheries project, is very funny."

My hands in my pockets curled into fists. I was jealous. Again.

I stepped away from her, seeking some distance and relief from the pinpricks along the side of my body.

"He'll be giving us the tour tomorrow," she said, again with that bright smile. That eager face.

"Great," I said. "Isn't this your room?"

We stopped beside a door with a pink ribbon tied around the knob. Her old trick. I touched the edge of the ribbon, letting it trail over my palm in a way I couldn't let her hair or her skin or any part of her body touch me.

Let this go, I thought.

Let her go.

"That was a good night," Brenna said, leaning against her door.

"The king is going to help us. That scientist you like so much will be coming to Vasgar next year to hold a conference with our fisheries experts. It will be a joint effort between our countries. I'm not sure how we'll pay for it, but we'll figure that out later."

A slow smile spread across her face. "You just...did that?"

I nodded, smiling at her smile. Refusing to look at the way she was standing and what her posture did to her body. The curves it revealed in her simple black dress, the perfect skin of her neck, and the sharp edges of her collarbones above the trembling rise of her breasts.

Okay. I looked.

"The king and I had a conversation," I said. "He's eager to help and we need it. Apparently he offered my father the same deal, but my father said no."

"I'm sorry," she said.

I smiled at her and for one long moment I let my imagination unspool. I let myself imagine putting my hand against the door beside her hair. I imagined leaning into that body, into those lush curves and soft skin. I imagined how she would gasp, how her eyes would widen with surprise.

But she wouldn't really be surprised, because she felt this as much as I did.

She wanted this as much as I did.

It was the Brinmark boat all over again.

It was like standing on the edge of that cliff. Feeling like I knew what I was in for but not having any idea.

Not really.

"Gunnar," she breathed. An invitation if I'd ever heard one. She even had her hand on the doorknob and I knew in two seconds we could be in her room. Alone in the dark. "No one would know," she said.

God, wasn't that the sterling heart of this moment? This temptation? It was just us in a foreign city. No press. An empty hallway. A different palace.

But the risk for her was too high.

I stepped back, shoving my hands back into my pockets, not that I'd been aware of taking them out.

"Good night, Brenna."

CHAPTER 13

T HEN
Brenna

WHEN I WAS young I had a bully. A kid named Marcus. His father ran the pub in town, which gave him a kind of royal status, which even as a thirteen-year-old boy he recognized and abused. Anyway, he had his sights set on me from the first day of school. Every day it was something with him, some kind of laser focus on the parts of myself that I felt most awkward and awful about. My boobs, mostly.

When it truly felt like I couldn't take it anymore, I complained about it to my mom, who in her casual way made it a million times worse.

"It just means he's attracted to you," she said as if I'd won the lottery. As if she were suddenly very proud of me. "He likes you."

This? I thought, dreading school. This is liking me? How awful. I wanted no part of it.

And as I walked to school that day, I got angrier and angrier. How dare that asshole torment me because he didn't know what to do with his feelings? I didn't have to take that. And since I'd tried ignoring him and that got me nowhere, it was time to deal with it.

Sweaty hands curled into fists, I found Marcus near the edge of the soccer field where he hung out with his royal court of jerks with patchy mustaches and unchecked BO.

And I ran—figuratively—right at him. I told him this was an awful way to try and show me he liked me. That all he did was make me feel bad. And scared.

He postured and said terrible things to me as I walked away, but then it was over. He focused his awful attention on someone else and I'd learned one of the most important lessons of my life: saying the thing that no one wants to say out loud gives you a kind of power.

That lesson had served me well at school and would undoubtedly serve me well for the rest of my life. It was like a super power.

Except for last night.

Swear to god, I'd thought we were on the same wavelength. Standing outside my door it seemed as if I could taste his desire. Because I had been drowning in mine.

But running right at it and saying the words we couldn't say out loud only seemed to push him away.

No one would know.

And still he walked away.

It was a windy bright day as we toured the harbor and offices of the initiative. Sven led us around, breaking difficult concepts down into layman's terms. Gunnar walked beside him, listening intently. Asking all the right questions.

While I was entirely preoccupied with thoughts of the

previous night. Had I read the signals wrong? It seemed the most logical answer, but I was totally unwilling to believe it.

"Brenna?" It was Sven next to me, his bright red cheeks matching the checks in his scarf. He really was a very nice guy. Exactly one hundred percent my type.

But even as we chatted, I glanced around for Gunnar. A habit I could not break at this point. And found him talking to two other scientists, but watching me.

Why didn't you stay last night?

"Sorry," I said to Sven, tearing my attention from a man who should not have it. "I was just thinking."

We turned to keep walking along the edge of the water. We were in a narrow inlet a few kilometers from the main harbor and all its hustle.

"It seems I'll be coming to your country for a few months," Sven said carefully. His eyes were on the dark green of the water as if counting the fish he couldn't possibly see.

"I've heard. That's absolutely wonderful."

"I look forward to seeing you," he said, smiling at me and then away.

He likes you.

It was my mother's voice in my ear. I heard it loud and clear.

And part of me wanted to put my arms around his feelings. So I could feel them, too, for him. Because he made sense.

But the other part of me was looking for Gunnar over his shoulder. Aware, deep, deep in my belly, that every time I looked for him he was looking for me, too.

Two hours later we were loading back onto the jet, the ink

on the deal between Sweden and Vasgar drying in my brief-case. I collapsed backward onto the banquette that had become mine and he took off his overcoat and suit jacket before sitting down in his. The narrow aisle down the middle of the jet was nothing, really. One step. Barely a step. And I'd be on his side of the plane.

But it was a line and I was going to stay on my side.

If a move was going to be made, it would have to be his.

"Can I get you something before takeoff?" Derek, the flight attendant, asked. A handsome man who, like a magi-cian, seemed to have everything we could ever want stowed away in some secret drawer on this plane.

"Akvavit?" Gunnar asked, smiling at me. "To celebrate."

"Sounds perfect," I said, kicking off my shoes. "And some of those nuts?"

"Of course," Derek said and went off to his secret stash of hard-to-find booze and spiced nuts.

"Wow," I said, slouching in the seat.

"We did it," Gunnar said, rolling up his sleeves. Gunnar rolling up his sleeves had become a kind of striptease to me. Some highly charged show of wrist and forearm. I glanced away, my hand on my stomach, trying to pull myself together.

"You did it," I said.

"Team effort."

Our attendant arrived with the traditional tall glasses for akvavit and a small bowl full of spiced nuts. The bottle of akvavit was plunged into an ice bucket in the armrest of Gunnar's banquette.

"We'll be taking off in five minutes," Derek said and I got busy buckling in and Gunnar got busy pouring drinks. The flight attendant vanished into his little room where he would wait until we pressed the button asking for his help.

The privacy was a terrible temptation.

"A toast," Gunnar said, handing me a tall glass. I was so awkwardly aware that our fingertips were going to touch, that there was no way they couldn't touch, that I nearly dropped the glass.

"Sorry," I breathed.

"No problem." He lifted his own glass.

"To fisheries?"

"We can do better than fish," he said.

"To the future of Vasgar?"

"Not quite."

"To future kings?" I said with a smile.

"I like that. But it's still not right."

"Then you make the—"

"To you."

I shook my head. My heart felt like it might pound right out of my chest and my stomach was alive with butterflies. Hyperaware butterflies.

"To the best team I've ever been apart of," he said. "Us."

He touched his glass to mine and then shot his akvavit back. His eyes locked on mine as the roar of the engines filled the cabin. I didn't drink my shot.

"What is happening between us?" I whispered, because I knew he couldn't hear me. I had to say the words. They were burning me from the inside out, like live coals in my throat. It was say them or burn up.

"I'm sorry," he said. "Did you say something?"

I shook my head, a coward, and downed my own drink. The akvavit's icy cold extinguished the hot words in my throat and made its way down my throat to my belly where its chill turned into warmth.

"Another?" he asked, the bottle lifted and dripping onto his pants leg.

"That's probably a bad idea," I said, wanting so badly to press my finger against that damp spot on the dark wool of those pants. I wanted to push my finger against the water drop until I felt the heat of his leg beneath it. The strength of the muscle. I wanted to press my palm against his leg to feel that muscle fill my hand. I wanted to slide my hands up his legs. Over his chest. I wanted to press myself against the hard planes of him. The terrible idea of him.

He poured us each another shot.

"Here's to bad ideas," Gunnar said, his voice low. Or maybe that was just the now-quiet hum of the engines as we lifted up and into the air.

Not committing, I held my glass so he could clink it with mine and he shot his back.

"That scientist," Gunnar said, leaning back against the banquette, one arm stretched across the back of the seat. His shirt was open at the neck, revealing a tattoo he'd gotten in the last year. A tattoo I'd never seen in all its glory. When I ran into him in the hallway when I first moved to the palace before the wedding, there'd been no tattoo on his naked chest. Only sweat.

Suddenly, terribly, I wanted to see the whole of the tattoo. I wanted that shirt off his body.

I guzzled the akvavit and looked away.

"Brenna?"

"Yes. Sorry. What did you say?"

"The scientist."

"Sven. He'll be a part of the team coming to Vasgar in the spring."

The muscle in his jaw popped out against the skin for a second, like he was chewing his tongue. Grinding his teeth.

"What about him?" I asked.

"Will you be excited to see him?"

I was surprised at the question. Well, perhaps not so much the question—I was aware in a very distant way of his jealousy. I felt it pulsing alongside my terrible interest. But I was surprised he was asking the question. The question felt like a door we should not go through.

He shook his head. "Never mind. It's none of my business."

"I'm not interested in him. Like that."

His eyes flew to mine and the air was so charged it burned up all the oxygen, and I was sitting there, not moving, but panting. He said nothing although his blue eyes burned me. Burned through my clothes. My skin. Down to the heart of me. The truth of me. Where this desire lived like a dragon waiting to be found.

And the question I shouldn't ask was suddenly in my mouth.

"Why didn't you come into my room last night?"

"Don't be foolish, Brenna."

"I'm not. I swear I'm not. I just...I've never felt like this. And I know you feel the same. I know, Gunnar. Let's at least be honest with each other. I can lie to everyone else, but not you."

I was wet. Between my legs. Without being touched or kissed or held in any of the ways I'd learned I liked. I just sat there, four feet away from him and that tattoo and those eyes, and I was ready. Wanting.

He set his glass down on the arm of his banquette. "Tell me to stop," he said.

"Stop what?" I whispered.

Graceful and predatory, he shifted forward, braced his hands on either side of my legs. I pressed them closed, dying for his touch, but the years of wariness and awkwardness were long ingrained.

"Tell me," he whispered, "to stop."

He inched forward and I realized he was going to kiss me. He was going to cross the line between us and we would kiss and everything would change. All of it. My entire life.

"Tell me," he said. His breath moved over my lips, he was so close. So close. And in a flash, I did the math. The careful calculations. The destruction versus the desire. We could never go back if we did this thing. It would live between us for the rest of our lives. He was going to be king. I was his stepsister. I would, at some point, have to watch him marry someone approved by the council. Arranged. Because it could never be me. And that would hurt. I could feel it already, the sharp sting of jealousy. The ache of not being good enough.

He nodded and leaned back, taking my silence as some kind of answer. "You always were smarter than me," he said. But before he could lift his hands away, I grabbed them. Held them, surprised by how rough they were. Delighted deep in my belly, where I was liquid and weak, that they were so big.

I clenched his fingers, and after a long second, he clenched mine. So hard it hurt, but the pain was right. The pain was just right.

"Say it," he said.

"Don't stop."

CHAPTER 14

THEN
Brenna

HE FELL to his knees in front of me, not just crossing the line. Owning it. Making it his. Leaning forward until I had to spread my legs as best I could in my skirt to give him room. It was awkward and strange. I felt trapped and stupid.

And then he kissed me. His hands cupped my face and his lips were on mine and it was... surreal. And perfect. I put my hands to the long lines of his jaw, the sharp edges of his cheekbones to feel the scruff of his beard. I was suddenly overwhelmed by the reality of it. Of him.

Of us.

At long last...*us*.

His fingers eased from my face to my hair. When he pulled it loose from the low ponytail I was wearing, the fine hair caught and tugged, a sweet, sharp sting that made me gasp against his lips.

He moaned low in his throat and his tongue slipped inside my mouth. His hand cupped the back of my head, lifting me toward him, shifting me the way he wanted. Holding me there as the kiss changed from careful to plundering. To ownership.

He kissed me like it was his last chance. Like it was now or never. And I got caught up in the fervor of it. The wild emotion of it. I pulled myself against him. He pushed up my skirt, getting it out of the way until his hands were on my ass, pulling me even closer. Even tighter.

There was no way to slow this down. We were an avalanche racing towards disaster.

Rough I pushed my hands through his hair until I was holding his head the way I liked. Our mouths open. Breath panting.

"Fuck, Brenna," he breathed,

"Yes," I said, over and over again. Yes, to him. Yes, to everything.

He worked on the buttons of my silk blouse and that seemed like a great idea. Exactly right. And I did the same. Getting his shirt out of the way, my hands on all that skin.

"Gunnar," I breathed. A question and permission. A reminder maybe. I wasn't sure. My brain was short-circuiting.

"Brenna," he whispered back at me, like we had to keep reminding each other who we were. Or maybe we were reminding ourselves because this seemed so incredibly unlikely. So entirely not like us.

I got his shirt open and leaned back, my hands sweeping down the corded length of his neck, over his smooth shoulders. Pushing aside the shirt that blocked the tattoo.

The wild wolf and the sword. The Vasgar Crest.

He leaned back a little. Looking down as if seeing it for the first time, too.

"It's beautiful," I said. The work was impeccable. The wolf seemed alive, the sword a real threat. Our country's coat of arms had never been so majestic.

I put my hand over his heart, over the wolf's snarling face. And he covered my hand with his. And it seemed, in this charged, volatile moment, like we both took a breath. Eased back.

"Maybe—" I said, but the rest of that sentence—*Maybe this is a mistake? Maybe we should slow down? Maybe we should pretend this never happened?*—was swallowed by his kiss. The sweet press of his lips against mine. All that heat banked. Careful. His hand over mine against his chest.

"Don't stop," he said. In his voice was a plea. One I'd never expected, that was just for me. A vulnerable moment that tipped me right out of sense. Right back into this madness.

"Never," I said. Stupid words. Nonsense, really. But, god, how I meant them in that moment. If he would have me, I would never stop. Always. Forever.

We were gone again. Wild and hot against each other. Fighting our clothes. Fighting each other to see who could get the other naked first. His shirt was off his shoulders, thrown against his seat. My shoes were gone. My blouse hanging from my wrist.

"My god, Brenna," he said, palming my flesh through the nude silk of my bra. I was not without some pride and it had taken me a while to come to grips with them, but I had killer boobs. I arched into his touch a little and he groaned, dropping his head against my skin. Running his lips, the scrape of his beard, against the tender tops of my breasts. He ran the tip of a finger, beneath the cup of my bra, pushing it down until the strap fell off my shoulder, hung drunkenly against my arm. The dark red of my nipple appeared and still he kept pulling until the bra was caught beneath my breast and I was held suspended and offered to him.

"You're gorgeous," he said, and I flushed hot and slowly, my hand on his elbow pulled him closer. And closer. Until he smiled. His dark chuckle making me light-headed.

"This is what you like?" he whispered. His lips finally, oh, thank god, finally against my skin. "This is what my shy Brenna likes?" He was teasing me, running his mouth, with its promise of heat and damp and suction, against my skin.

"Gunnar," I whispered. Part plea, part chastisement.

His hand cupped my breast, the nipple, hard as a stone, caught between his fingers where he applied a subtle twisting pressure. But it wasn't enough and I pressed myself forward on the bench seat until his waist was between my legs. Until I could feel the heat of him through my stockings. Until my breasts were pushed up hard against his chest. But he stopped me, held me at an impossibly tiny distance that shouldn't matter, but did.

Soft kisses landed against my skin. Everywhere and nowhere at once. Maddening kisses. Pressure, but not nearly enough. Heat, but not nearly enough.

I moaned and arched and still he held me distant, until the moans turned into growls in my throat.

"Tell me," he whispered against my lips. Not kissing me. Not really.

"Gunnar, don't be a tease."

"A tease? Me? It wasn't me in those shoes today, Brenna. Walking around in those shoes that turned your ass into a wet dream. Walking around in those shoes, hanging on the words of that scientist. It wasn't me laughing at everything he said last night, with my hand on his shoulder. It wasn't me against that door, so pink and flushed and perfect and so...fucking...ready."

My eyes opened and narrowed. "It wasn't me," he said. "Looking over his shoulder every ten minutes to make sure I was watching."

"You were, though, weren't you?"

His face was flushed, his eyes dilated, and I couldn't tell if he was angry with me or turned on. Or both. My guess was both. Because I felt the same way. I wanted to kiss him and bite him at the same time.

"You think I was ready for you last night?" I asked.

"I know you were." So imperious. So sure.

I shrugged, like maybe I was and maybe I wasn't.

He laughed, low in his throat. "You were ready last night and you're ready now. I can feel you against my stomach. You're hot and you're wet, Brenna. For me." He leaned forward. "I can have you any way I want you."

I surged forward, snapping my teeth at him and his eyes widened. Surprise and dark delight. "Like that, then?" he whispered.

"Fuck you," I said.

His hand dropped my breast and I made a move as if to stand. To push him back and get to my feet. But he grabbed my face in one hand, my hand in the other, pressing my palm down against the soft fabric of the seat.

"It hurts," he whispered. "Doesn't it? Wanting so much."

I clenched my jaw shut and he pressed a kiss to my mouth. One soft one. A peck and then another. And I sat there, mutinously. Shaking with my anger and my desire.

"I know," he said. "Because I feel it, too."

"Then do something about it." I pushed up against him. The hot and damp part of me that pulsed and ached. I pushed and pushed, looking for some relief. "Please," I nearly sobbed. And something in him snapped.

He bent his head, found my nipple with his mouth. Pulled and sucked with a force that hurt at first and then became just right. I cried out, clutching at his head. "Oh, my god, yes. Gunnar. Yes."

He pulled me by the waist until I was nearly off the seat and he continued sucking at me while his hands tore at the zipper and buttons of my skirt and then my nylons. He tore and ripped and shoved until finally it was just the black silk of my underwear, the bra under my breasts, and me. Pale and pink and panting under his touch.

"Fuck," he said. "Look at you." With one hand he pushed me back until I was reclined in front of him. Probably not a good angle, but I didn't care. I was so far beyond caring. He ran the flat of his palm over me, from my collarbone down across my breasts to my waist, until finally his hand slipped over the silk between my legs.

He ran his thumb over the wet spot he found there. Over and over again, as it grew. Touching, just barely, my clit and then down again.

"More," I said.

"What?"

"Everything."

"This?" He slipped that thumb under the edge of the silk, groaning when he pushed into me. "Brenna. My god."

I rocked against him. Mindless. Wanting. Desperate. "Gunnar."

"I should have known you'd be like this," he said. "All or nothing. Demanding your due."

"I haven't even started demanding," I said with a laugh.

He grinned and rewarded my audacity with a finger. His thumb brushing through the damp curls to find my clit. I bowed off the bench seat. Strung up on electric currents originating from his tricky fingers. I braced my bare foot against his thigh, twitching and jerking as his thumb worked me and his fingers filled me.

His other hand was on my breast again, finding that pain that turned so quickly to pleasure.

"Oh, Gunnar. Don't. Don't fucking stop."

He didn't. He got up on his knees, bending over me so he could watch me as I came. Whispering, as I did, filthy, impossible things.

"You're so fucking perfect like this," he breathed. "I'm going to keep you coming. I'm going to keep you just like this. Wet and hot and fucking begging for me."

The orgasm was a flash fire. All-consuming and then gone. Or banked perhaps. Waiting for another chance to roar and rage. I sat up a little, kissing him as I did it. Pushing away the hand he still had buried inside of me. Working a clit that was numb for the moment.

I reached for him, the flat of my hand against his belt and then the hard length of him behind his pants. Oh, god, he was...perfect. I felt the fire begin again. The coiling in my belly.

Kissing him I worked the belt and then the zipper. I had him in my hand when he stopped me, breaking the kiss. He put his hand over mine, forcing me to stop touching him.

"What?" I asked.

"Brenna."

"What?" I kissed him. And kissed him. Willing him to stop whatever silly game he was playing. But he tore his mouth away.

"Brenna. Enough."

I flinched at his sharp words. His commanding tone.

And then I just sat there, blank. Wondering what was going on and what had changed.

He did up his zipper. The sound of that metal closing did something to my spine. "Is something wrong?" I asked, and he didn't answer. He only crouched there, breathing deep. Not looking at me. Something was happening, something I didn't understand, and I tried to pull myself together.

"Did..." I swallowed. "Did I do something wrong?"

"No," he said. "No, not at all. You..." Finally he looked at me, and whatever he saw made him look away. His jaw clenched.

I waited an embarrassingly long time for him to finish that sentence and then I realized that he wasn't going to. I shook my head, not wanting to believe what I was thinking.

"I don't understand what's happening."

"We're done. Stopping."

"Is this... a game?" I asked. I closed my legs so I was no long spread before him. I felt myself, swollen and hot and wet. How fucking embarrassing. How perfectly fucking me. Giving so much more of myself than anyone really ever wanted. "A trick?" I asked. I found, by some miracle, my shirt and shrugged into it. My hands touched my breasts, sore and abused, and I flinched. Eased my bra back into place. I would feel all of this tomorrow.

Every humiliating moment.

He was silent and still looking away from me, so I filled up all the silence myself.

"Let's find out how desperate Brenna is? Let's find out if you can make her beg?" My voice cracked over the word *beg* and I struggled to get to my feet. I had to get away. Away from him. Away from the smell of sex. Away from the echo of all my words and his.

I'm going to keep you like this. Hot and wet and begging for me.

He said that. He actually said that.

"Congratulations," I said, choking and miserable and scrambling for my pride. "You win."

CHAPTER 15

T HEN
Gunnar

THIS WAS another moment I should have let her go. Let her leave thinking the worst. The wedge between us so immutable there would be no recovering from it. No chance we would ever cross the chasm.

But she was near tears.

And she could believe the worst of me. It would probably be better if she did.

But I couldn't let her go believing the worst of herself, too. I couldn't have her embarrassed by the way she gave herself to me. The way she wanted and desired and demanded and finally came.

But I also couldn't fuck her.

Trust me, no one was more surprised than me.

She got to her feet and I caught her hand. Still not

looking at her. I was trying, for fuck's sake, to do the right thing. I couldn't do the right thing and look her beauty in the face.

I was, after all, just a man, and not a very good one at that.

"Let me go," she demanded in a frost-burned voice.

"Sit."

"Fuck you, Gunnar."

"Please."

She struggled against me, and I grabbed her by the waist and pushed her back onto the seat. Brenna was strong and she was pissed, but she wasn't going to win in a physical fight against me. And she knew it, so she sat there and crossed her arms and her legs and she looked at one spot over my shoulder.

And as I watched, she lifted a fist to brush away a tear that clung to her eyelashes.

God damn, I was a fucking monster.

"I didn't go into your room last night because it would have been a mistake."

"And this wasn't?"

"No, it was. This shouldn't have happened," I said.

She laughed so hard it sounded like a sob. And her face was turned so far away the tendons in her neck stood out. I could see her heartbeat. I watched her swallow.

"Look at me."

"Fuck you."

"Brenna."

"You can manhandle me all you want, asshole, but you can't have everything." She swallowed hard and then shook her head. And I knew what she was thinking. Because I was thinking it, too.

I would have given you everything.

I sat down next to her and she pushed herself away so fast, the feel of her against me barely registered.

"Please...listen."

"You've not given me a choice."

"I'm going to be married, Brenna." That made her look at me, her mouth open, eyes wide.

"Has it been announced?" she said through pale lips. "Are you engaged?"

"No," I said. And she sagged, relieved that she hadn't fooled around with a betrothed man. God, her honor, even now, was diamond bright. "But I will be."

"In a few years."

Remarkable that her words stung. That she didn't care that I would belong to another, as long as it wasn't soon, when the thought of her looking forward to seeing Sven again filled me with a black rage. It would be sooner than that. Far too soon for both of us. "I won't sleep with you, Brenna. And marry someone else. Our lives are entwined forever. My wife will be your sister and I can't...disrespect you that way. Or her."

She laughed incredulously and I flinched, unprepared for her biting humor when I was being as honest as I could be.

"Are you trying to tell me you're being noble?"

"Brenna," I sighed.

"Now?" she asked, getting shrill. "This moment. How incredibly convenient for you."

"Nothing about this is convenient," I snapped.

"Or true," she snapped back.

"My marriage," I said. "Will not be of my choosing and I can expect very little from it. Not happiness. Not passion."

"Let me go." She struggled against me and I pulled her down until we were face-to-face. Too close. I felt, all too keenly, the heat of her against me.

"I want you," I whispered, as honest as I'd ever been in my life. "But I can't have you. I can't know how you taste and smell. I can't know what you feel like from the inside. I can't make you come and let you touch me and then...forget it."

"I don't want you to forget it," she said, no longer spitting. I could see her begin to believe me and I looked away, letting her go.

"You are so important to me, Brenna," I said. "I can't make you less so, just so I can get laid."

She was burned into my brain. I looked down at my chest, surprised somehow that the shape of her wasn't imprinted there.

"Maybe you won't have to marry," she whispered.

"You know I don't have a choice, Brenna. I will be the king of Vasgar. And Vasgar is broke."

I could feel her gaze on my face and I was too much a coward to meet her eyes. Too afraid that, even though I knew what was right, I would ignore it. For more of her.

"I've never...been so turned on and sad at the same time," she whispered, and I laughed with no humor. But there was nothing I could say. I didn't know how to change my life.

"We shouldn't have done it. But I'm glad we did."

"All right," she said, and I felt her shift, leaning forward to kiss my cheek, and I eased away so she couldn't. Because I was hanging by a wire.

"I'm sorry," she whispered.

"I know. Me, too. I just...need a minute."

She gathered her things and slipped by me, making sure

we didn't touch, which I didn't want to appreciate as much as I did. The door to the bedroom clicked shut and I blew out a long breath. I lifted my hands and inhaled her scent. Pulling the musk of her deep into my brain. My lungs.

Doing the right thing fucking sucked.

CHAPTER 16

T HEN
Brenna

I REFUSED TO AVOID HIM. I refused to pretend I was sick or to miss the weekly meeting with the council members in the library. I looked him in the eye as best I could and pretended so well—so completely—that nothing had happened.

At times I almost believed it myself. Convinced myself that the plane ride hadn't happened.

And then our eyes would catch across the Viking table, or I'd hear him laugh at something Alec said or I'd catch the scent of him, and the plane ride would roll back over me.

The way he knew so exactly how to touch me, stroke me, send me reeling to the moon.

And then I would have to remind myself all over again that he was not mine.

I could not have him.

Every night I spent panting into my pillow hoping my own fingers would chase away the memory of his. But it never worked, and soon it seemed like my room was haunted by memories of him, even though he'd never been there.

That's how persistently I thought of him. How impossible he was to forget.

Early morning breakfast was still my sanctuary. The coffee was hot, the spiced rolls fresh, and no one but me would be there for hours.

Which was why, when Gunnar opened the door just after I arrived on Friday, I jumped to my feet.

"Gunnar."

"Brenna." He was so startled he didn't move, and the ornate door closed on his shoulder. He pushed it back and stepped inside. We'd taken such care this last week to never be alone, to never tempt fate. And this was the dining room, with servants coming in and out, and his father and my mother might arrive at any moment.

But the nature of being alone with him made none of that matter.

He wore a thick grey sweater and black jeans. His hair, usually pushed off his face and held in place by some kind of product, was loose and swooped down over his high forehead.

He looked like a handsome man. A very handsome man, but just a man. Not a prince. Not a star terribly out of my reach. Just a guy.

"What are you doing here?" I asked.

"My dad wanted me to meet him."

"He's not here."

"No. I see that."

My fight-or-flight mechanism kicked in hard and I

started to gather my laptop and paperwork. It was a hard choice between the spiced roll and the coffee but I went spiced roll.

"You don't have to leave," he said, watching me gather myself.

"That's okay. I can work in the library."

My arms were full and I was doing all I could not to look at him, and I certainly didn't want to touch him, so I stopped a foot from him. My eyes focused on the edge of his chin where it met the soft, fuzzy neck of his sweater.

The memory of his beard against my skin sent a physical pulse through me.

I nearly dropped the spiced roll.

"I miss you," he said. A murmur, a breath I felt more than heard.

"What do you mean?" I asked, playing stupid. "We've been in meetings all week."

"I miss your mouth," he said and I flinched. "I miss your breasts. The feel—"

"Don't. You can't—"

"God damn it!" The door slammed open again and the king came barrelling through. Gunnar stepped forward, ushering me out of his father's way, which only led me back to the table.

"What the hell, Gunnar!" King Frederick shouted and slammed a folded-up newspaper onto the table. "I have to hear about this fisheries business through the god-damned newspaper?"

"We sent you a briefing," I said, and both Gunnar and his father stared at me. "We did. I called your secretary a few days ago to see if you had questions."

"What is happening?" the king asked, looking between

us. "You and your assistant planning to take over the throne?"

The assistant bit was nothing but bait and I rolled my eyes.

But Gunnar jumped.

"No, Father," Gunnar barked. "Brenna and I are trying to get our country out of the financial tail spin that you have only made worse! The fisheries initiative is right. It's the right thing to do and you're only angry because you didn't figure it out."

King Frederick went pale and then red. Gunnar and I shared a quick look, suddenly alarmed that this fight might turn into something much more dire. "Sit down, Dad, you know your heart can't take this—"

"Don't you dare tell me what I can take or not. You are a boy. Playing at being a leader. Playing at being king." Frederick stepped toward Gunnar and the air smelled like trouble. "The newspapers are calling you the saving grace of Vasgar. Tell me, Gunnar, how are you going to pay for this saving the fisheries?"

"We can figure it out."

"Oh." The king looked mean and proud, and he looked over at me. "How much will this fish project cost?"

"Five million the first year."

The king laughed. "Five million! You think we have that lying around? You think that's just something we're going to figure out?"

"If you'd let the oil investors invest the damn money, this wouldn't be happening!" Gunnar shouted.

"I have a few ideas," I said, stepping into the smoking war zone between father and son. But none of them would get us five million dollars and the king looked at me like he knew it.

"You're getting married, Gunnar."

Gunnar shook his head, his jaw made of stone. "No. Not yet."

"The American heiress has agreed to the terms."

I tried not to react, not to stiffen or suck in a pained breath. But I did all of those things.

"Terms?" I asked in an empty voice. What terms?

"When?" Gunnar asked. Blowing over my question like he already knew the terms.

"Does it matter?" the king asked, his voice silky and terrible. "Tomorrow. A month from now. You're marrying the heiress."

I glanced up and our eyes, for one heart-stopping second, clashed. I'd spent two weeks not looking at him, or at least not the whole of him. Looking, if I had to, at his hands. Or his chin. Never his eyes. Scared, perhaps, of what would happen if I did. What I would reveal. How I would lose another part of me.

When our eyes caught, even in front of all the people we needed to hide from, I could not stop myself from feeling everything I wasn't supposed to feel. My longing for him was like hitting a brick wall. I flew into it so hard, I broke.

Gunnar broke eye contact first, looking back at his father. And I felt like all my strings had been cut.

"The heiress may have agreed," Gunnar said. "But I have not."

"Because of her?" the king asked, and it took me a second to realize he was talking about me. I felt myself go numb all at once, like being dropped in freezing cold water.

"No," Gunnar said, so fast and with such conviction that I believed him. "Because we're not there yet. We still have time."

"You have until the Winter Solstice Festival."

The king smacked the paper down again and then, like nothing happened, like he hadn't just reordered the entire universe, he walked over to the buffet and picked up one of the sweet rolls.

Without a backward glance I was up and out of that room, laptop in hand, sweet roll forgotten. I had no sense of Gunnar behind me, not until I was outside my door, panting and sweating and trying not to cry—or trying not to admit that I was crying.

I opened my door only to have it slammed shut by Gunnar's hand. He was behind me. His breath ruffled my hair into my face. I bent my head and gave myself a second to feel him. One weak, awful second to just soak myself in the warmth of him. It was all I could do not to press back against his chest.

So weak. All I wanted was that one second. He could marry the heiress but I could have this second.

"Go away," I demanded close to collapsing. "Please."

"Let me in."

I shook my head because if I opened my mouth again I would sob. If I opened my mouth again I would beg him to touch me.

"Brenna," he breathed and reached down and put his hand over mine on the door handle. And I didn't stop him.

I would think about it for years, how in the end it wasn't really Gunnar I could blame for everything that happened after he opened that door.

It was me.

Everything that happened. The way it all came apart.

It was my fault.

CHAPTER 17

T HEN
Brenna

THE DOOR CLICKED SHUT behind us.

"Did you know in the airplane?" I asked. "About the heiress? The winter solstice?"

"No. I knew it was inevitable. But I didn't know my father was going to go over my head."

I believed him. Perhaps I shouldn't have. But I did believe that.

"I'm sorry this is happening to you," I said, my back still to him. The world outside my window was bright blue. Endless. And I put all my energy into staring out that window. Like that blue sky and the one fluffy cloud, the wheeling seagulls, were the only things that mattered.

But still, I heard him move. I could feel him behind me. Long before his hand cupped my shoulder. Before he said, "Brenna, I swear I never wanted to hurt you."

Oh, god, he didn't even know how it hurt. How I ached. And burned. How my skin was too tight. And my lips stung with the memory of his kiss. I tried, night after night alone in my bed, to diminish the memory of his hands between my legs, using my own. But it didn't work.

My touch only heightened my longing for his.

I was sick with it.

"Go away," I said.

"Brenna," he groaned, like the idea was just too painful, and I couldn't sit in this limbo with him anymore. Wanting but not having him.

"Go away," I said and turned, stepping close enough that our panting chests touched. "Go away or make it better."

"How? Tell me how," he said. He wanted me to tell him how to get out of the marriage. How to be a king and be with me. And there wasn't any way to make that better. It was impossible.

But that also wasn't what I was talking about.

"You said on the plane that it hurts to want so much. And it does, Gunnar. Make it better."

His eyes flared and then narrowed.

"Do it or get out." I threw down the gauntlet with all the thwarted anger I was battling. And Gunnar picked it up in the same fashion. His arms around me were rough. His kiss —oh, thank god, his kiss was even more so.

But I fought back, wanting more. Wanting every bit of this unruliness, this pained desire. Our mouths were open, eyes closed. I clutched him to me, holding him as hard and as close as I could.

"You want it like this," he said, between biting, sucking kisses that left me reeling. Drunk.

"I want you anyway I can get you," I said. He groaned

and wrapped his arms around my back, lifting me up, my feet dangling inches off the floor.

He kissed and kissed and kissed me, walking the whole time to my bed. He dropped me on the white sheets, splashed with bright squares of summer sunlight coming in my windows. I sat there, my legs splayed, and he stood beside the bed, looking down at me with his red lips and an erection straining behind his jeans.

"I've always thought you looked like the epitome of summer in Vasgar. Bright and warm—"

I didn't want compliments or poetry. I didn't want words that felt good now but would sting the day after the winter solstice. I wanted to get fucked. Until I didn't care what came next.

Looking him in the eyes, I put my palm against his cock, pushing the heel of my hand harder and harder until he grabbed my wrist. All that romance vanished from his face.

Good, I thought. We won't survive romance.

"It's like that?" he said and didn't wait for my response. He crawled up on the bed over me and I lay down, first on my elbows and then on my back. He crouched over me, dark and thrilling, and my entire body was thrumming with electricity.

"This is a mistake," he said.

"Probably. But I don't care."

And then it was on. We kissed like treasure was buried in our mouths. Under our tongues and behind our teeth. He put his hands in my armpits, scooting me up on the bed so that we were facing each other.

With frantic fingers I unbuckled his belt, shoving his pants down until I could get my skin on him. Until the thick long curve of his erection filled my hands. He gasped though his teeth like it hurt, just a little, to have me touch him. And I liked it.

This should hurt.

And then it was his turn to make me hiss and cry, his fingers under my blue shirt. He lifted it up over my head, tossing it into the corner of my room. My hair fell down over my face and I pushed it back with my arm in time to see him bend over me, kissing his way down my stomach.

"Don't—" The breath came out of me before I could stop it.

"Don't what?" he asked, pausing. Looking up at me from the other side of my breasts.

I stared at my ceiling and hated my insecurities. We had a real porn scene going here and I'd ruined it.

"Just...hurry." I pushed my skirt down over my hips. It was one of those stretchy ones with no zippers and I'd never been so fond of a piece of clothing.

"I'm not hurrying," he said, kissing my stomach again. The small fold of skin under the edge of my bra. The shimmying curve of my lower belly. Oh, I hated it and I pushed him away, or tried to, but he was having no part of it. He was as moveable as a rock.

"I know what you're doing," he said, kissing my belly button. "And I won't let you."

My hands flopped beside me and I sighed. The petulant teenager I'd been. He chuckled against my skin. His hand slipped beneath my underwear. I gasped as his fingers found me below the silk.

"You're beautiful, Brenna. And I'm going to prove it to you all day long if I have to."

"We have meetings..."

"Cancel them."

I laughed.

"I'm not joking."

Fuck. It.

I combed my fingers through his hair and then reached down to the hem of his sweater, pushed up by his slow slide down my body. He lifted his hands just long enough that I could get the sweater off him. The mussy hair left behind was so sweet I took a second to pat it down, sweep it up out of his eyes, but it only slipped back down.

"I want to see the tattoo," I told him, and he rolled to the side of me, propping himself on his elbow. I scooted down a little until I was eye to eye with the wolf.

"It's beautiful," I said, tracing the edge of the sword.

"Thank you," he said.

"Why did you get it?" I asked.

"So I wouldn't forget again," he said. "Who am I and who I serve."

Right. Of course. I was only borrowing this man. And, with apologies to the American heiress, I would be borrowing this man until I had to return him.

But what if I didn't...

That soft voice was trouble. I knew it even now. But it was insidious and it did not stop.

What if I could convince him that I was better for this kingdom than the heiress? Better for this kingdom than any other woman the council would try and force him to marry? Sure, she had money. But I had plans. I had vision and with me at his side – we could rule the country the way it should be ruled.

Because I was better for him.

I closed my eyes and pressed a kiss to that wolf. To the smooth skin of his chest. To the beat of his heart. And I kissed my way down to the skin that wasn't tattooed. To his lower belly, which trembled at the touch of my lips.

"Is this really happening?" he asked and I glanced up at him.

"Do you want me to stop?"

"God, no. I just...I've put a lot of mileage on this fantasy, I just wanted to be sure it was real."

He grinned down at me and I decided, then and there, this would be the best blow job in his debauched life. Not that I knew if I could deliver on that, but I'd make an A-plus effort.

I'd done this a handful of times, always slightly embarrassed by how badly I wanted to do it, but then once I was there, face to...er...dick, I was suddenly uncomfortable with how intimate it was. And how lost I felt. Like there were no clear instructions.

In porn it seemed like I just needed to shove the whole dick down my throat until my eyes watered and I gagged. How that was hot, I didn't know. In romance novels, it seemed like a couple of careful licks would put the guy suddenly on the very edge of his control.

There was so much territory between those two places.

I held him in my hand, ran my thumb over the dark red head of his dick. He was so soft there, and damp, and the more I did it the damper he got.

And, frankly, the damper I got.

And he made these sounds. Not groans or anything, but these soft inhales every time I stroked him and I liked that. I liked that a lot. And I wanted to see what he would do if I licked him. When I leaned forward and did it, he groaned and the sound set off a kind of chain reaction in my body. My heart felt like it might burst through my ribcage. I took him in my mouth and his hand cupped my head, his thumb stroking my jaw and, god, how I liked that. I squirmed on the bed, taking him deeper and deeper. Listening to his breath saw through his chest. His fingers clenched in my hair and he ground out between his teeth, "Fuck, yes, suck that dick."

I suddenly understood why this was different. Why I wasn't uncomfortable. Because this was Gunnar. Because I was invested in turning him on. In making him feel as good as he could stand. Every sound he made was a clue. The way the muscles of his legs twitched and clenched told me a story about his control. His fingers in my hair, against my jaw, alternately clutching at me and patting me.

All of it. I loved all of it and I wanted more.

Because I loved him.

"Brenna?" he said and I realized I had stopped. His dick in my hand. My head turned just slightly, like I'd heard a distant sound.

I love him.

"You okay?"

Yes. Maybe? Stupid. I was absolutely stupid, falling for this man. I believed in the best of him, but even I under-stood loving him was asking for future heartache. He was imperious and temperamental. Privileged and elitist. A boy, really, in a man's body.

But he was also kind. And hardworking. Self-sacrificing in a way that I never expected. He was compassionate and smart. And he fought. He fought really hard, with tools he wasn't very good with yet. And he took his lumps and learned his lessons and kept coming back for more. That perhaps was the most loveable thing about him. The most honorable.

And he was sexy as fuck.

"Baby?" He sat up, curling over me, turning my head so I faced him. "What happened? Did you hear something?"

Future shattering of my heart, but I'd worry about that later.

Now was for him. And me. And the deep longing that felt like an ache and a joy all at once.

I kissed him. I kissed him with lips that burned from being stretched around his dick and I pressed myself full tilt against him, feeling the beat of his heart against the beat of mine.

"Please," I said.

"Yeah." What he agreed with I wasn't sure. I wanted to believe all of it. The longing that hurt and the love that I couldn't say out loud.

"I don't have a condom," he said.

"The Playboy Prince doesn't have a condom? Someone should tell the *Times*."

"I haven't been with anyone since you moved into the palace."

"Two years ago?" I didn't want that to mean anything, because it couldn't.

But my heart raced and throbbed and my face went red with the pleasure of that statement. With everything my hungry heart could interpret it to mean.

He shrugged. "I stopped buying condoms."

I reached over and pulled my purse from the cozy chair where I usually threw it when I walked in the door. "Convenient for you," I said. "I've done the opposite."

"Been with a lot of other guys?" he asked, and I could tell he was trying to joke, but it didn't really work.

"Just...Daniel. But he wasn't why I started buying condoms." I lifted the package. "I bought these for Helsinki."

He kissed me softly. Breathing in and out. His hand

feathered down over my hair and to my back. "You're amazing."

"You are, too."

He shook his head. "I don't know how I convinced you of that, but I'm glad you think so. I'm glad...you're letting me touch you. Even if it's just this once."

I nodded and kissed him back with my lips closed tight, because there were too many words that wanted out.

"Open that condom, princess," he whispered against me. "I need to be inside you."

I grabbed the box and pulled out the small swath of silver-wrapped condoms. I tore one off and handed it to him, dropping my purse back over the side. It was a caveman trick, what he did, getting up on his knees over me and ripping the wrapper with his teeth, the muscles in his stomach and arms flexing.

And I loved it.

He bent and kissed my belly. My breasts. He licked my nipples, making me gasp. All as his fingers slid up my thigh to cover my pussy. "I can feel you," he whispered against my breast. "I can feel how hot and wet you are. You make me crazy, princess. You..." He shook his head. "You make me so fucking crazy."

"Hurry," I said, arching up into him. I circled his wrist with my fingers, urging him to be less careful, and he took me at my word. Slid his fingers up into me until I gasped.

"Fuck, baby," he groaned, his forehead on my belly as he watched his hand and my body. "I can't hurry. I want this to last forever."

His words weren't helping. They were stones I added to my pockets so I could sink deeper and deeper into my disastrous feelings.

His thumb stroked my clit and I pushed aside all my

worry about what would happen next and just let myself be here. And now. With this man. He stroked me and filled me and I clutched his back, the oncoming orgasm twisting me tighter and tighter. I bit his shoulder and muffled my cries, and just as I shattered—my body flung up high into the stardust—he pushed himself inside of me.

There was no controlling my wild scream or the bowing and twitching of my body. I saw stars and then more stars as he stroked in and then out of me, his hands on my waist, holding me earthbound. Holding me where he wanted me.

Finally I came down, sweating and spent, to the bed where he had me pinned.

"Oh, my god," I breathed, because it was the only thing I could do. I couldn't lift my arms, or push my body back against him. I could only lie there and feel the slow in and out of him. A tide I had no interest in resisting.

"Brenna," he said, and that was all, my name on a loop, groaned between his teeth. And my hazy brain finally took him in, finally saw him. Chest heaving, every muscle straining, sweat dripping from the tips of his hair down onto my body. I lifted my arms to his shoulders, stroking him.

"Come," I said. "Please, come."

"One more for you," he gasped, slipping his thumb back between our bodies. And I could have told him that it wouldn't happen. Or, at least, it never had before; two orgasms were impossible. Especially after one like the first? There'd be no way I'd come again. But his thumb stroked my clit and he watched me with silvery, wolfish eyes and it was there.

The tension in my belly. The spark.

I let him work me—work both of us—back into some kind of state, frantic and animal.

He braced himself over me and I grabbed his wrist, turning my head to bite his hand. He swore and laughed.

"Me, too," he said. He felt the same way. Like he was barely holding on to himself.

"Please," I said. "Come."

And I knew he wouldn't come without me and so it was a frantic driving fuck now. I was pushed nearly off the bed. My legs up over his shoulders. His head bent to mine where he whispered endless nonsense. And I whispered it back. We were sweaty and wiping it all over each other.

"Yes!" I said. "Yes!" And I let myself go. Exploding up and out of my body, out of my head. And he came with me. And we were together and it was the best I had ever felt in my life. Effortless and primal. I was just feeling and sensation and a wild out-of-control love.

My breathing slowed. But my heart didn't. I feared my heart never would.

"You okay?" he asked a few seconds later when he could speak. When he'd caught his breath, when the skin of his chest and face had faded to something not quite so red. I couldn't stop touching him, my hands slick with sweat over his shoulders and back.

"So good."

"Yeah," he said, smiling down at me. "Me, too."

And we lay like that, smiling at each other, sweat cooling on our bodies. And this big thing was happening around us, and in us, and I felt myself changing.

I could only hope he was changing, too.

CHAPTER 18

T HEN
Gunnar

IT WASN'T A MISTAKE. Being with Brenna felt far too important to be a mistake. Far too real in my life that had been full of shallow and fleeting things. But it was definitely a bad idea.

Ill-advised.

Because it was going to end in heartbreak. Even the best-case scenario—she got on a plane to live her life far away from me and this kingdom, while I married a wealthy woman who would not love me and who I could never love —well, it sucked. Hard.

Every night I meant to break it off.

We'd spend the day pretending that nothing was going on, and maybe I was delusional but I believed that we did it so well that no one knew. Not Ingrid or Alec. Not our family. Not the public that was starting to follow my every move.

Every day we worked hard. There were meetings with the minister of energy who was so deeply in my uncle's pocket that even talking to him was a waste of time. But Brenna didn't give up trying.

Every Tuesday she went to his office for a meeting, laying out the case for less and less foreign involvement in the offshore drilling. And every Tuesday he all but laughed at her.

I visited the army base in Ildag, where I had done my own basic training. We had a small but fiercely proud military in our country, honed by years and years of having to defend our shorelines against those who would control us.

Our secret council meetings grew by first one member and then another.

And every night, in the quiet of the castle, I crept along the stone hallway from my room to hers. Every night before I pushed open the door to her room I had stern words with myself.

You have to stop. This can't go on. We'll be found out.

But then I would open the door and there she'd be. And it didn't matter what she was doing, or what she was or was not wearing, it was her.

Brenna.

"Hey, baby," she would say, and all my good intentions to end it with her would die on the vine.

We had two months like this. We didn't talk about the future. I believed she was still planning to go the UN and the deadline with the heiress was charging at me a million miles an hour.

I had lived my life firm in the knowledge of one thing and one thing only—I could not have what would make me happy. It wasn't even a consideration. I'd known it as a child, as a teenager with a love of music and dreams of music school in Vienna, and as a young man with a father he could never, ever please.

I knew I could never have Brenna, because Brenna made me happy.

And I thought she understood that. That our mutual heartbreak had been agreed upon at the beginning, because we did not live normal lives. But I should have known Brenna was going to fight for herself.

For us.

And damn everything else.

CHAPTER 19

Now
New York City
Brenna

NEW YORK CITY was too loud for me. Too bright. But from the back of the limo I couldn't look away from the window. All that neon was hypnotic and alarming.

"I assume you have some reports I need to look over," Gunnar said, settled in next to me, so close I could feel the electricity from his body like the electricity out there in the night. I forced myself not to shrink back, to hold my space. To fill up my space. I was no longer the shrinking girl hiding in the back of that library. "Or are you going to catch me up to speed yourself?"

I pulled an iPad from my leather briefcase and handed it to him.

"Thanks to money from an American investor group, we were able to diversify the foreign investment in the oil drilling—"

"An American investor?"

"Came to us through Donal. He vetted him and was the go-between—"

"This...group...you don't know who they are?"

I shook my head, watching the city in neon pass by my window.

"Nope. The first installment paid for the fishery project. And then it grew. I've tried to push Donal for a meeting or even a name. But Donal is a...vault."

"I remember," Gunnar said.

That's right. The meeting that summer in Aberdeen. I had forgotten that lunch.

"Our budget is balanced for the first time in twenty years. We have doubled down on renewable resources, particularly wind. We're building turbines on Tyre."

"That won't bother the sheep?"

I smiled, only because I was sure he couldn't see me. "The sheep don't seem to mind. We've committed forces to NATO. As well as renewed our monetary pledge. And we've taken in two thousand refugee families. We're committing more money toward financial aid for students who want to study abroad."

"What about farming?"

I turned. "Farming is in decline."

"And you're not worried?"

"Of course, I'm worried."

"That you're sending our young people off to Scotland and Sweden to get an education and they won't come back?"

"But the ones who do will be educated, and they'll help our fishing and agricultural centers flourish."

I turned to face him, surprised to find him watching me.

"It's everything we planned," I said. "In the library three years ago."

"You made it happen," he said, and I looked away.

"The money helped." I was uninterested in his approval and didn't believe his reverence.

"I still can't believe you stayed."

"And I can't believe you left."

I'd been working my tail off while he'd been sitting in the basement of some club fondling women in spandex. Using his reputation to sell vodka, of all things.

His approval meant shit.

"Read the report. You have a lot to catch up on," I said.

The interior of the car was silent as he read and I continued to look out the window, the snow falling in thick white flakes to melt on the glass.

"Had things gone differently this would have been your home," he said. "New York. The job."

"It never would have been my home." Already I missed the mountains and the snow. I even missed the wind. "But how fitting that it's become your home," I said. "All this light blinds people to any number of sins, I imagine."

"Yes, and I have done my best to exploit them all," he said rather predictably.

"What's going to happen to your bar?" I asked after a few minutes.

"Bars. Plural. I own three and two restaurants. As well as some apartment buildings in Brooklyn."

"You have a kingdom of your own, it seems. You worked fast in three years."

He smiled with half his mouth. "I bought most of the properties before I left."

"You were planning this all along?" While I'd been imagining us on the throne together, he'd been planning to leave Vasgar?

"Everyone needs an escape route."

"Not me," I said defiantly. Even as I had several planned for the next few months. Oh, what a hypocrite I was.

"You have to sell them," I said. "The bars. You can't—"

"I know."

"Will it be hard? I mean...did you like it?"

He shook his head. "It was just nice to have something of my own, you know? Something that had nothing to do with my father."

"You can make Vasgar your own."

"You've already turned things around," Gunnar said, lifting the iPad. "The work you've done. It's amazing. More even than we'd dreamed."

"Thanks," I said, shooting him a quick smile, weakening despite all my efforts. I looked out the window, burning my eyes on all the light.

"Have you ever been to New York before?" he asked as the car drove us through the neon night.

"Why?"

"You've got that wide-eyed *I've never been to New York before* look on your face."

"That's a thing?" I asked, smiling reluctantly.

"It is."

"It's just...how much money does it cost to keep the city lit up like this?"

"More than our gross national product for ten years."

"Do you like it? The city?" I regretted the question as soon as I asked it, but as his silence went on and on I turned to find him staring out his own window, his face pensive.

Don't care, I told myself. *Do. Not. Care.*

"I missed home every day," he finally said. And I stiffened at the longing I heard in his voice.

"Banishment was your choice."

"Yes," he said. "It was."

That was how badly he didn't want to be with me. He'd left the home he loved to live in the middle of this garish island, as far from me as he could get. I knew it was more complicated than that, but that's how it felt. In the dark night in my bed.

It felt like he'd never wanted me at all.

Because it had been so easy to leave me.

"Well, it worked out for you, didn't it?" he asked. The words were cutting but his tone soft.

That was the nature of Gunnar. And I'd chosen, years ago, to believe his tone and not his words. And it had been a mistake. Now I would hear his words and ignore his tone.

"I'm not interested in slinging mud with you, Gunnar. You've been sitting on a false throne in the bottom of a nightclub. I've been trying to save your country. I owe you nothing."

"You're right," he said after a moment. "I'm sorry."

I narrowed my eyes, waiting for the next blow. Because Gunnar did not apologize.

"And thank you," he said, catching me off guard. "Thank you for taking such good care of the country. It could not have been in better hands." He pressed his hand to his lips and then his heart, a common salute in our country. A sign of respect.

I looked back out the window, not believing his tone *or* his words.

CHAPTER 20

T HEN
Vasgar
Brenna

"GUNNAR," I sighed and kissed his shoulder, the warm, smooth skin stretched over hard muscle. I kissed it again, because how could I not? "You can't fall asleep." One more kiss for good measure. And that little dip of tendon, the thrilling change of terrain where shoulder met arm—that needed a kiss, too.

"I'm not sleeping," he said, his deep voice rumbling up from the pillows beside me. His hand fished out from beneath me to grab his phone from the bedside table. He tapped at the phone's face and the light of the clock illuminated us in green.

"What time is it?" he asked, his head still buried.

"After three."

"Wow. That's...that's gotta be a record." He'd snuck in here a little after midnight.

I laughed, blushing and embarrassed, but thrilled, too. I kissed the inside of his elbow because it was so pale and tender and his.

"Keep doing that and I definitely won't be sleeping."

He shifted in the bed, and the sheets we were tangled in released the warmth and smell of our bodies. Of sex.

My bed smells like sex.

I found that pretty freaking delightful.

And that it smelled like sex with Gunnar Falk? Well, that was still a dream I hadn't totally processed yet. I slipped toward him on the sheets, curling my body around his. If three hours of sex wasn't a record, maybe four would be.

"Hold it there, princess," he said, turning to face me, his sliver-gray eyes half-lidded and sleepy. God, he was sexy.

He propped himself up on his elbow, and the wolf tattooed in beautiful detail across his chest shifted as he moved. Like it, too, was restless and wanted to howl.

They really were works of art, the tattoo and the chest. Two months of him in my bed and I still wasn't used to him.

"You really need to leave," I said. "We have a council meeting in, like, five hours."

"I have lunch with the foreign ministers today, too."

"Do you need help?"

"No. I got that handled."

Good, because I hated the foreign ministers' meetings. And he knew that, which might have been why he let me off the hook. The foreign ministers were old men in the same vein as the king and his brother—they didn't like dealing with a woman.

I couldn't resist one more kiss, to his lips this time. Full and soft right now, but capable of twisting into cruel smirks and cutting smiles. It had been a while since they'd been directed at me but I'd bet the foreign ministers got plenty of them.

"Though I'm not leaving until we talk," he said.

"Now you want to talk?" I laughed. We were whispering, and the bed felt like a cocoon. The palace intrigues, my mother and his father, and all the gossip and scrutinizing and judgment. They had no place in this room.

"I came in here to talk," he lied. "You distracted me." His hand slid down over my hip.

"Okay," I said. "Let's talk. You keep your hands to yourself." I pushed them back toward his body.

"And you keep your lips to yourself."

"Agreed. Go." I grinned at him and he grinned back. My miles of blond hair were spread out against the pillows, the ends of it tangling with his jet-black hair.

"I have to see the heiress next month."

And just like that I was ice cold. The soft slippery want of a minute ago froze solid.

"And I think you should take that weekend to go to New York. Pick out an apartment. I have—" He grabbed his phone and it was only because he wasn't looking at me that I had the courage to say what needed to be said.

"I've refused the job."

He paused and I closed my eyes, reading so much danger in that stillness. The beginnings of a fight I had to believe wouldn't end us.

"Why?" he finally asked, turning to stare at me with wide, angry eyes.

"Because..." I couldn't put it into words. Not yet. I could only lift my hand and sort of circle it around the bed. His eyebrows lifted and his soft lips got sharp edges.

"No," he said. "No, Brenna. You're not giving that up for me."

"Listen to me. Hear me out."

He sighed, my lover vanishing as my old nemesis returned. Stubborn and cutting. This wasn't how I wanted to do this.

"There is so much work that needs to be done. Work that you're doing. That we...*we* are doing. We have put the plans in place to grow our economy, to strengthen our schools—"

"So you're skipping a job with the UN to *work* for me?"

Ah, I could not say I had no pride. Because that stung.

And this...what I was proposing...it was all pride. He wasn't wrong. Some of the ideas we were working on were mine, and I loved my country enough and I...I loved Gunnar enough to want to lead alongside him.

"*With* you. We could..." Oh, it was hard to say, even if I was proposing it as a business venture. A *do what's best for the kingdom* kind of deal. But I knew he would see right through it to my soft beating heart behind the idea.

I didn't have to say the words, though; his mouth fell open for just a moment in the most horrible shock. I could not look at him and see his horror at the idea.

I had thought... Foolish. Stupid Brenna. He'd never said a word about love while he was between your thighs.

"Marry?" he asked. "Are you proposing to me, Brenna?"

"We would be good for Vasgar," I said in a small voice.

"Not as good as the heiress."

Whether or not he wanted to hurt me didn't matter. He wanted to remind me. And it was possible he didn't know how I felt about him. I felt like I broadcast my love every minute of every day, but maybe he really didn't know.

"That's not true," I said. "And you know it."

"What part of Vasgar is good for you?" he asked. "Not your mother. Not my father. The council led by my backward misogynistic uncle. The palace gossip. Why would you want that when you could have the world, Brenna? The whole goddamn world and any part of it you want?"

"I only want this part." That did not come out as strong as I'd hoped. "And you."

He rolled off the bed, sitting on the edge with his back to me, and I fumbled on my bedside table for my glasses. Once they were on I sat up and pulled the sheets from the bottom of the bed where we'd kicked them. I pulled them up over my body, which suddenly was flawed again.

Thick Brenna, wanting more than I should have.

I felt a shuddery kind of pain start in my chest. Like everything was breaking apart.

And I did what I always did—I ran right at it, because if it was going to break, I was going to break it into a million pieces.

"I love you," I said to his long, lean back in our ancient language. "And I want to marry you. For the country. And for...for me."

He was silent for a long time, his head bent, his dark hair flopped over his forehead, damp with sweat.

"Gunnar." Hope and love made a fool of me. "Are you going to say something?"

"You know we can't. It's impossible."

"Why? Because your father says so? Because—"

"Because I'm the goddamned prince, Brenna! Because my entire life has been about marrying someone who would save Vasgar."

"But we're doing that. Together—"

"We're playing Brenna. We're playing at saving the country. Because for any of this to work, we need money. A lot of money. Money that will only come from my marriage."

"There are other ways," I said.

"Name one."

I didn't have one. I didn't have any. Maybe he was right. Maybe we were playing.

"If I marry someone with no money, the first thing my father and uncle will do is sell the oil rights. And everything we've worked for will be for nothing."

He stood and turned to face me, proud in his nudity. His muscles and tattoos, the flaccid length of his penis against his leg. I blushed looking at it, even now.

"Can you get the job back?"

"I don't want the—"

"Can you get it back?" he roared, and stunned, I nodded.

They'd said if I changed my mind there would be a place for me at the UN.

"You can?" His relief broke my heart.

"Yes."

He started to pull on his clothes. "Then you'll call them as soon as it's reasonable. You'll call them and you'll get your life—"

"Don't," I said. "Don't do that. Don't pretend you know what's best for me."

"You want to stay here and watch me marry the heiress? Maybe you can do a reading during the wedding, that bullshit Corinthians quote. Maybe I'll set you up as my mistress, is that the life—"

"Don't pretend you don't feel something for me. Like I'm living some fantasy."

"Sweetheart." The smile he gave me was not...the smile I'd grown used to. The one he gave me across the throne room or in council chambers, the sly, secret, sweet one that I'd believed had been just for me. No. He gave me his cruel smile. The ruthless twist of his lips that he'd greeted me with when my mother and I had moved into the palace and he'd hated me.

"Don't," I spat. "Don't do that. Don't turn the last two months into something awful."

The smile fell from his face and now...now he just looked sad.

"You just proposed to the future king of Vasgar and you don't think you're living in a fantasy? You're my stepsister, Brenna. The scandal alone—"

"We can figure it out."

With sad, distant eyes he looked down at my soft white body. The shape of me obvious under the sheet. My too-broad shoulders, my too-big hips.

A peasant's body, my mother always said when we went to try on clothes that never fit. My father's blood.

"Gunnar," I breathed, trying to find a blanket to pull up over myself. The sweat gone and replaced by a chill so deep I could feel it spreading to my bones.

"You are not meant for the throne of Vasgar," he said.

And then he, the man who'd taken off all my clothes, kissing every body part revealed, pulled the duvet up like he was tired of looking at me.

"I will marry the goddamned heiress," he said and pulled on the thin silk pajama pants he'd worn into my room. "And her money will save this country and cement my control. And you—"

He looked down at me on the bed and I scrambled up and out of it, the sheet clutched to my chest. My heart breaking into a thousand pieces. "You'll get that UN job back and you'll get the fuck out of this country if I have to fly you there myself."

"I don't want the job, Gunnar."

"Listen to me, Brenna." He leaned over the bed. "Listen

very carefully, because I will not say this again." His eyes looked all over my face, as if pulling apart each piece of me for dissection and disposal. My pink cheeks. My glasses. My blue eyes. My heavy eyebrows. My long blond hair.

"Get on with your life," he said. "Marry some nice man and have a nice life." The way he said *nice* was condemning. "And the fact that your peasant mother married my father will be a footnote in your history. A story you tell at boring dinner parties."

And he left. He just left, and I stood in my bedroom in the palace that had just begun to feel like home, and I was too hurt to cry. Too broken to sob. I could only, and with great effort, keep my heart beating.

CHAPTER 21

T HEN
Brenna

I DIDN'T CALL to get my job back. In my shaken, furious state, I couldn't even imagine that conversation. And I was sure Gunnar would apologize. The day passed and I didn't see him, and I waited in my room that night, sure, absolutely sure, my door would creak open and he'd come in contrite and worried about me.

But my door stayed shut that night.

And the next night.

For a week of nights.

And then, finally, I gathered up the courage to sneak to his room, which I found locked. And I knew in the broken corners of my whole body that he'd done that. He'd locked me out. I knocked, and after a long moment the door opened. Gunnar stood there, cold and removed, and I knew,

I knew this was useless. He'd already built the walls to keep me out.

Locked all his doors.

"Don't do this, Brenna," he said, and I'd never in my life felt so desperate. So small.

"I just want to talk."

"Did you get the job back?" I didn't answer. "Did you?" he snapped and I was startled into shaking my head. And I had to come to grips with the reality that it didn't matter if he loved me or wanted to be with me.

He was going to fall in line with what his father and this country demanded of him, without ever seeing what else he could have.

"Get the job back," he said and shut the door.

And for a moment I was comforted by feeling bad for him. By feeling just a little superior to him.

But it didn't last.

"What is wrong with you?" my mother asked, when I walked into the dining room for breakfast. It was later than I usually went and I hadn't been paying attention or I wouldn't have braved the room or my mother, whose eagle eye saw everything. And she could not stop herself from commenting.

It was raining out, which was perfect. The high windows were full of gray clouds and raindrops. "You look awful."

"Thank you, Mother," I said, taking my coffee to sit in my usual spot at the table. The walls were hung with portraits of the royal family stretching back hundreds of years. I felt all their eyes watching me. Judging me.

But none of them more so than my mother.

"Would it kill you to wear lipstick? A..." She dropped her voice, though no one was in the room with us. "A proper foundation garment?"

"Good morning to you, too," I said, pulling my chair in until the heavy spruce table bit into my stomach. I wore a long sweater over leggings—a tent, really. Hiding all my flaws. My mother had been putting me in Spanx and girdles since I was ten and didn't understand my preference for being able to breathe.

My mother, of course, looked perfect. Thin and regal, like she'd been born in the palace instead of a shitty fishing village on South Island. She'd been plucked from her life as a single mom and bartender by the king when he made his tour of the island five years ago. He'd taken one look at her and decided she would be his new queen.

Now look at us.

So much for the fairy tale.

"Seriously, Brenna, don't you look in a mirror?" Mom asked.

"I don't care, Mom," I sighed. I didn't have the energy to fight with her. I was braced, waiting for Gunnar to come in. My entire body caught in a flinch I could not let go of.

"No," Mom said. "You don't care. You've never cared how your actions reflect on me. How they reflect on the royal family."

"Do you honestly believe that the fact I'm not wearing lipstick to breakfast matters at all? Are you that shallow?"

The door to the family wing of the palace banged open with such force the portraits rattled on the wall.

"Too far!" King Frederick bellowed, lurching into the room, leaning hard on his cane. He needed a wheelchair but he was too proud for such things. He looked gray and shaky.

His hair and beard were a wild bramble around his head. "You've gone too far, Gunnar."

"Have I?" Gunnar asked, strolling behind him.

If I looked messy and unkempt, he looked...I swallowed a too-big gulp of coffee. Perfect.

He'd started wearing dark pants and dress shirts with the sleeves rolled up. It made him look like he was ready to get something done. It had been Ingrid's idea and, as usual, Ingrid was painfully right.

"You'll have to fill me in, Father. I'm afraid I couldn't guess which of the things I've done lately have gone too far. Was it the school visit or the—"

"And you!" Frederick spat, pointing a shaking finger at me. I was too shocked to do anything but sit there with my mouth agape, but Gunnar dropped that sardonic, uncaring smile and his entire face focused. "I always knew you'd be an embarrassment."

"What...?" was all I could manage while my mother put her head in her hands.

Frederick slammed a paper down on the table. Gunnar grabbed it and whatever he saw made him go white and then red. And his eyes, when they met mine, were full of apology. And anger.

Whatever it was, it was bad.

"Let me see," I whispered. Gunnar shook his head, but I got to my feet and grabbed the paper out of his hands. It was a photo. A grainy cell phone picture of two people half-undressed, making out.

On the private jet.

It took me a second, unused to seeing myself like that. Head thrown back in ecstasy. Clutching a dark-haired man's head to my chest. But the headline made it real clear.

Bad Boy Prince and Porky Princess Keep It In the Royal Family.

THEN
   Gunnar

IT WAS ALL I could do not to touch her. Not to pull her into my arms and tell her that it didn't matter. That the world had it all wrong.

In front of me, her head bent, Brenna sobbed.

Or gagged.

And I couldn't touch her. Not in front of my father. Not when she needed to get as far from this place as she could. If this wasn't proof that this island would diminish her and stifle her power, then what was?

I grabbed the paper and crushed it in my fists.

"You can't do that with every paper," she whispered.

"We'll sue them."

Her chuckle was damp with tears she wasn't going to let fall.

"It must have been...?" she whispered.

"Yeah." Derek, the attendant. He was fired, to say the least.

"You are out of control, Gunnar! You have no respect for this country, for the throne or our name. You never have!" Father bellowed. "But this...this is a new low, even for you."

"Frederick, please calm down," Annika begged. "You're going to send yourself to the hospital—"

"Look at the paper, Annika! Look at the shame our children have brought us."

Brenna wobbled and I couldn't stop myself from

reaching out to comfort her. God, how I wanted her. I'd never *longed* in my life. Or if I had, I'd been too young to remember it now. But I *longed* to comfort her and be comforted by her. But she stepped away.

Annika uncrumpled the paper and blanched. Brenna looked away, her eyes wet with tears.

"What about the shame *you* have brought to this family?" I asked my father. A swing he didn't see coming.

"Do not change the subject!" he yelled.

"You are selling this kingdom out from under the very people you are supposed to protect."

"So noble, Gunnar," Father sneered. "Were you this noble while fucking Brenna in the jet—"

"Shut your mouth, old man." I grabbed him by the front of his shirt. Ready to take every moment of pain Brenna was feeling out on him.

"You are stepping very close to treason, son. You know how our ancestors handled treason?"

"You going to put me out on the glacier? I'd welcome it," I spat.

"No," he said. "But the two of you will get married."

"No," I said. Out of the corner of my eye I saw Brenna flinch. God, I hated myself right then. I hated every minute of my weakness that had led us here. "Absolutely not."

"There is no *no*," my father said. "You'll get married."

"I'm willing," Brenna said.

"We won't be getting married," I said to her, pleading with her to see what the old man was doing. "Because that is exactly what he wants, Brenna. He wants us to marry so that I won't marry the heiress. So I won't bring in new money, and he and my uncle will be able to sell the oil rights to Russia without anyone protesting."

On her face I saw the penny drop and I'd never seen someone hurt so much.

I wanted to tear off my own skin.

Dad was silent. And smiling.

"Tell me I'm wrong," Gunnar said.

"I'm the King of Vasgar," he said. "I don't have to tell you anything."

"If we marry," I said to Brenna, every mistake I'd made littering the ground around me like shattered glass. Stupid. I'd been so stupid. The first rule of my life had been not to underestimate my father. He'd probably paid the flight attendant. "He gets what he wants. And everything we've worked toward is ruined."

"We can figure it out," she said, clinging to the idea of us. "Like we have all summer long. We can do this."

I was envious of her will, but we did not have the luxury of hope.

This, I thought, this was the terrible collision we'd been heading for. Not the last two months in her bed. Not the scandal and the destruction of her reputation. But this—the moment when I finally stopped pulling my punches. When I used my sharpest barb against her soft heart and reminded her of the truth she'd forgotten about.

Brenna deserved so much more than this broken-down kingdom and my father and his cruel palace.

She deserved more than me.

"We could do it," I said. "But I don't want to. I don't want *you*, Brenna."

Annika gasped. Brenna stared at me, white and trembling. The words slowly...slowly sinking in. And I didn't look away. I didn't flinch. I stared at her until she realized I wasn't bluffing. I watched her until she believed what I was saying. Until the love she felt for me curled away in pain.

I watched her until she turned her back on me—believing the very worst.

It was the only way to break her heart.

"Then you'll leave," Father said, and the whole room went still. Silent.

"You're banishing me?" I asked. "Is it official? Or just another threat?"

"You have embarrassed this family enough with your indifference and disrespect. You have crossed the line. I can't have you in this palace. She is your stepsister."

She is the best thing to ever happen to me.

"Excellent," I said. I would figure this out somehow. Manage my father's power and my uncle's greed some other way. From some other place.

"Wait!" Brenna said, her hands out like she could ward off disaster. "Gunnar is going to be king. He needs to be here. We don't have to get married. I will leave, but Gunnar needs to be here to—"

Save the kingdom.

"I'm not dead yet," the king said with his usual pride and no small amount of victory in his dark eyes.

I'd done this. I'd made it so easy for him to win. I was sick with shame and regret. What a fool I'd been, thinking I could win. The fight was never fair with my father.

But he had no idea how dirty I could get.

"And my brother can inherit the throne," Dad said.

Brenna gasped and looked pleadingly at me. My uncle was worse by a million times than my father. And if allowed, he would destroy this country. And I wasn't going to let that happen, but I also couldn't tell Brenna that. Because she would make us into a team again. She'd find all my weaknesses and in no time I'd be powerless to push her away.

I took one last look at Brenna, knowing she only saw my

cold face. My betrayal not just of her and everything we'd worked for, but of Vasgar. And fine, she could think that if it would make her hate me enough to leave. And not look back.

"Go to New York," I told her, memorizing her face. "Leave this place behind. Lord knows I am."

"But Vasgar?"

"Leave it for the crows," I said, which was the one thing I could say that would destroy her illusions of me. "Go, Brenna. Go...be amazing."

And with that, I walked out of the palace, away from my country.

And the only girl I'd ever loved.

THEN

Brenna

THE KING HAD a massive stroke the day after Gunnar left.

I was in my room, pretending to pack instead of curling myself into a ball and questioning all my life choices, when I heard the commotion and my mother's screaming.

For a week the world was upside down. And about twenty times a minute I considered texting Gunnar. And twenty times a minute I resisted. The Gunnar I'd thought I knew...he'd respond. Despite how he felt about his father, the Gunnar I'd thought I knew would fly back. Because the country was in turmoil. The palace was in turmoil.

And I was, too.

The other Gunnar, the real one, I guess...I didn't know what he'd do. And I didn't feel strong enough to weather whatever response he might have. And, frankly, the fact that he had to have heard and hadn't reached out...well, didn't that tell me everything I needed to know about him?

"How are things today?" Alec asked, finding me in the back of the library where I was spending a lot of my time when I wasn't at the hospital.

"Frederick is coming home today," I said.

"That's good news."

I shook my head. The king and my mother hadn't allowed anyone to visit him. So no one knew the full extent of the stroke. "Between us?"

"Of course, Brenna. You know that."

"He can't walk yet. His speaking is..." I sighed. "Poor."

"The council is freaking out," Alec said. "I mean, they're saying all the right things about giving the king time to recover, but there's a lot of conversation happening in the background."

With Gunnar's Uncle Eric. The bastard was trying to get to the throne, using the stroke as his way in.

"How bad is it?"

"The council wants to talk about temporary leadership and I've held them off as long as I can."

"Can you get us one more week?"

He nodded. "I think we can do that. Ann is a good ally. I'll get her to keep everyone calm."

"Thanks, Alec," I gave him a smile and stroked my thumb over my phone out of sheer habit. He hadn't called. Or texted. Not that I'd expected him to, I just couldn't seem to stop myself from checking.

"How are you holding up?" Alec asked.

"Fine."

"I thought...you were leaving. New York and everything."

"I can't leave with everything the way it is," I said.

"Gunnar would want you to leave," he said quietly. "That's all he wanted."

"Oh!" The rage inside me burst out in a large and surprising laugh. "Well, lucky for the country, what Gunnar wants doesn't matter much to me."

"Brenna—"

I lifted my hand. "I'm fine. And I'm not interested in sympathy. Or your thoughts on Gunnar. It's you and me keeping the wolves at bay for as long as we can, okay?"

He nodded. His face so solemn under that red beard of his. Alec seemed to have lost some of his wattage when Gunnar left. Probably we all did. There was an outsized hole in all of our lives.

Why did we let him matter so much?

"I'm sorry I yelled," I said and he smiled.

"I'd hardly call that yelling," he said. "And I'm sorry... about Gunnar."

"You and me both." I sighed, shaking off the feeling that even talking about him gave me. "Does he know? About his father?"

"He knows." Alec didn't say anything else and I didn't ask any of the millions of questions burning on my lips. He knew and he wasn't going to do anything. He knew and he didn't care. How much more did I need to finally believe the truth of him?

Gunnar did not care about us. If Vasgar was going to be saved, we were going to have to do it without him.

ALEC, with help from our allies on the council, managed to keep the discussion regarding the king's ability to lead post-poned for two weeks. But it still wasn't enough time. Fred-erick was doing better. He was walking with a cane, but speaking was still difficult and the left side of his face was slack.

Convincing the country that he was still fit to rule would be impossible.

"Sir," I said, in the family dining room where I was sitting with my mom and the king. My mother looked like she'd aged a million years in the last week. She looked tired and thin and...hopeless in a lot of ways. The red lipstick she wore fooled no one. "We need to make a plan."

"What kind of plan?" Mom asked, looking at Frederick and then back at me.

"Gunnar," I said and the king shook his head.

"Sir—"

"Banished!" he said.

I'd expected this. For weeks he'd entertained no conversations about ending the banishment and bringing his son back. Which would be the easiest solution. And the best. But he shot it down every time.

Luckily, I had a plan B.

I pushed the documents I'd had drafted by Deena, one of the crown's lawyers, toward him.

"These are papers that would give my mother—" Mom looked up, stunned and scared. Not exactly the emotion I was hoping for. "Your wife, the role as your representative—"

Frederick shook his head.

"I would help her. You would too. Alec, Ingrid, everyone would help."

"No," he said and shoved the papers so hard they slipped right off the table.

Mom sniffed and looked away, drinking tea like it was all that mattered, but she was hurt. Hell, I was hurt. And mad. And frustrated.

"If you don't make a plan, your brother—"

"Fuck...him," Frederick spat.

"I agree with the sentiment, but with your illness and Gunnar being gone—"

"Not...dead," he said. His face turned an apocalyptic shade of red.

"Sir!" I got to my feet. "You have to calm down."

My mother sat in her chair, sipping tea as if nothing was happening.

"Mom!"

She laughed and shook her head. "Don't look at me. If he wants to kill himself, fine."

My god. I knew she'd gotten more than she bargained for with this marriage. More tragedy than joy. More problems than fewer. But the callousness of her not caring was breathtaking.

"Don't look at me like that," she said quietly. My mother was not going to rise to the occasion. And the papers I'd had drawn up making my mother a representative of the crown were useless. I should have known. I felt myself shrinking under the sudden pressure of the situation.

Someone...someone tell me what to do.

But the dining room was silent. The answers weren't going to come from here.

Right. I took a deep breath. "I'm going to go into that meeting," I said. "And I'm going to try and buy us some more time. But without a plan...your brother will convince the council that you are not fit to lead. And once he gets his hands on the throne...it's gone. And you know it."

Fredrick lifted a shaking hand to wipe at his mouth. But said nothing. Not one thing. He didn't even meet my eyes. Suddenly I was envious of Gunnar's indifference. How lucky to not give a shit. To not feel every moment of this pressure.

How lucky to not feel so alone.

It was me against the hordes and there was nothing but a cliff at my back. And Alec stalling for time in the council chambers.

Fine. I buttoned my jacket, hoping for inspiration. I'd worn a suit today, anticipating if not this scenario, one like it. Ingrid had helped me buy it. It was bright red and cinched tight at my waist. It was a power suit and I felt powerful in it.

But as I made my way from the family quarters, through the palace toward the council room, some of the power flaked away, leaving me raw and worried.

Why is it just me and Alec standing here? How did this happen?

I opened the door to the council meeting and found Ann speaking. Members of the council turned when I came in but sighed with disappointment when they saw I wasn't the king. Ann kept speaking and I sat in my usual chair against the wall.

The chamber had been updated since the days when men carried swords. There were long tables and comfortable chairs. AV equipment and microphones. Electronic voting machines. But there was still a huge fireplace along one wall with the skin of a giant wolf above it.

My country. In a nutshell. One foot in the present. One foot in the past.

Ann was talking about the council's ability to govern without a king. Without a leader. That they shouldn't make drastic changes in times of great uncertainty. That the council should make a joint statement saying they supported Frederick and that everything was okay.

I was comforted that most of the council was nodding.

Except for Eric.

He sat in his spot at the head of the council table. He

looked nothing like his brother. Eric was big where Frederick was slight. Full of bluster and a kind of destructive, bullying energy. I caught his eye and he smirked at me, confident I was outclassed by him.

I wanted to punch him as hard as I could, right in the face.

Alec sat next to me. His Viking size was wedged into a suit, too, and I wondered if Ingrid picked it out for him. It was quite dashing.

"Did he sign the papers?" he asked and I shook my head.

"What are we going to do?" he asked.

And quite suddenly I was laughing. I was laughing uncontrollably in council chambers.

"Pardon me," Sven, the council member from the northwest corner of South Island spoke up. "Brenna? You come with news from the king?"

"I do." I got to my feet and took my time walking over to the end of the table. "First, I want to extend my stepfather's thanks and appreciation for all your kind words and gifts. We, my mother, stepfather, and I, all appreciate the patience you've shown us as we've kept the doors to the family quarters closed. King Frederick gets better every day—"

There was a sudden commotion behind me at the door and my mom was there holding open the door, looking wide-eyed and worried.

He's dead, I thought. But then King Fredrick walked through the door with the help of his cane. His hair had been brushed, but he had not shaved and the council all gasped at the sight of him. Head held high, he made his way to where I was standing and I quickly shuffled out of the way to give him room but he grabbed my arm.

I blinked, startled and unsure. "What...what do you need?" I asked.

When he looked at me, I saw more fear than I could have guessed possible. He reached into his coat pocket with a shaky hand and pulled out the papers I'd had drawn up to give my mother power to stand in his stead for a very limited time.

Everywhere my mother's name had been it was crossed out.

And my name was written in my mother's handwriting.

The papers were signed by the king.

"You," he said. "You."

Slowly, I nodded. The enormity of this was more than I could fully understand. But there were dozens of eyes on me and time was moving with super speed.

King Fredrick turned towards his brother. "Not. Dead. Yet!"

"What's happening?" Ann asked.

My mother helped King Fredrick back to his seat and I turned to the council and explained very slowly, that, by his decree, I would be standing in for the king. For as long as it was necessary.

GUNNAR HAD BEEN RIGHT.

That's what I learned in my first six months as the woman behind the throne, trying to keep the country moving forward.

Gunnar had been right.

I hated to admit it. More than I could bear, I hated to admit that Gunnar had been right. All of our noble plans. None of them could help us pull the country out of poverty. None of them could save us.

I'd put too much stock in hope.

And fisheries.

"I'm not kidding," Ingrid was saying. The library was my office and the table in the back my desk. Ingrid had come back to Vasgar when I took the position at Frederick's side and she helped me in all things related to public relations.

And mostly she kept me from losing my mind on a regular basis.

"Look at him," she said, holding out a magazine she wanted me to see. The fire crackled behind her and a winter storm beat at the glass in the windows.

"I don't want to."

"He looks ridiculous," she said. "I mean...the throne and the fur cape? Who does he think he is?"

"I don't care."

Ingrid slapped the magazine down on the chair beside her. "You're the only woman in the world who doesn't want to make fun of your ex-boyfriend."

"He wasn't my boyfriend," I said. "And I'm too busy."

Donal had called asking for a conference call. They had an investor—a group of investors, it sounded like. And I trusted Donal, but I was not going to get fooled by hope. Not again. Clear eyes and a rational heart—that's what I needed.

And for Ingrid to stop messing around with gossip magazines.

"Can you look this over?" I asked, handing her my notes for the conference call.

"Sure," she said. "I'm just gonna go get a cup of tea. You want anything?"

I shook my head.

When she was out of the library I sat back in my chair and told myself to be strong.

You don't care, I reminded myself.

But I reached for the magazine anyway. First surprise...it wasn't a gossip thing. It was *Esquire*.

Hmmph.

The magazine fell open to the picture of him. And I could brace myself all I wanted but it did no good. None whatsoever. My heart squeezed so hard I actually gasped.

Gunnar.

And he didn't look stupid. Not at all.

He wore a crown and a fur robe, black with white trim. A pair of leather pants and nothing else. Not one other thing. Except maybe some tasteful yet dramatic eyeliner.

The tattoo was on full display. The abs.

He looked very *Game of Thrones*. Very Wicked Prince. Very, very much like himself.

He sat on a throne, his hand around the neck of a bottle of vodka. That half curl to his lips that was so familiar. The look in his eyes that told you he was in on the joke, but that it wasn't really a joke, was it? Being so masculine. So regal.

So impossibly sexy.

I didn't read any of the words. They didn't matter. The picture was going to sell a million bottles of that vodka.

He'd capitalized on his reputation. His family and country. He'd used us all just so he could leave us behind.

I threw the magazine in the garbage.

CHAPTER 22

Now
New York City
Brenna

I HATED TO SAY IT, but I had grown accustomed to the royal jet. I was spoiled. All these years I'd resisted, haunted as I'd been by the memory of Gunnar and I and that flight back from Helsinki. But if I never sat in the banquettes at the back of the plane and instead sat in the captain's chairs toward the front, if I concentrated on the soft, sweet leather all around me, the latte with just the right amount of sugar brought to me within moments...well, the ghosts did not bother me so much.

"Thank you," I said to Melinda, the head flight attendant.

"You're welcome, Ms. Erickson. And for you, Your Majesty?" she asked Gunnar.

"Coffee," he said. "Black."

Melinda nodded and was back in a moment, like the cup had been waiting for him.

Gunnar said nothing because he was used to this kind of treatment. And I'd never grown fully accustomed.

My phone binged and I checked the messages from my assistant. I had two more job interviews for Monday. Good. Fine. I put my phone away with a shaking hand.

"What's wrong?" Gunnar asked.

"Nothing."

"Your hands are shaking. Is it flying?"

"I'm not scared of flying, Gunnar, if that's what you're asking."

"You told me that story about flying out of Edinburgh in a storm."

It was my turn to gape at him, slightly stunned he'd remembered. I'd completely forgotten.

"I'd be scared to fly after that, too," he said with a shrug.

"As a representative of Vasgar, I've flown plenty," I said. "It's not that."

"You're not going to tell me why your hands are shaking?"

"I'm not going to tell you."

"All right," he said, swiveling in his seat, the iPad on his lap for the moment. He'd been glued to it for the last part of the trip. He'd asked a few questions that reminded me he'd been training to be king his entire life. And perhaps...he'd been keeping track of Vasgar. Not so willing to leave it behind, after all.

He'd have a learning curve, but the council would help him. The country would be fine.

I could leave and never look back.

"Can I ask you something else?"

"You can ask me whatever you want. I don't guarantee I'll answer."

"Excuse me," Melinda said, coming to stand in the doorway. "We will be taking off shortly. Please buckle your seat belts."

Gunnar shrugged out of his black cashmere coat and handed it to Melinda, who stood beside my seat waiting for me to take off my jacket. And for a moment—a split second —I was the naked girl on the bed. Rejected and vulnerable and so embarrassed by her body and her desire and her love. But I felt Gunnar's eyes on me and I wouldn't admit that he'd hurt me. Not for anything.

Not even the throne.

And fuck that guy. I was a goddess.

I stood and took off my coat, revealing the black pencil skirt and red silk shell I wore. It was rumpled and a little sweaty.

But there were more important things to worry about.

I took off the fur hat and handed it to Melinda before sitting back down.

When I crossed my legs at the knee, my silk stockings whispered against each other.

"What were you going to ask?" I lifted my latte and took a sip, arching my eyebrows at him over the cup.

He, however, was staring at me, mouth slightly agape, and I felt the blush I hated rising up along the bare skin of my neck revealed by the V-neck shell.

"Your hair," he said.

"What?" I asked, touching my hair, the intricate braids keeping all the long blond flyaways in place.

The braids were a ridiculous throwback to my Viking heritage, but I'd been clinging to them. The people seemed to like it. I did, too. It made me feel strong and powerful.

Connected to the fiercest part of myself. It was a crown of sorts. One I'd made myself.

"You look good, Brenna," he said.

"Don't—" I bit off the word before I said anything else. And then got busy clipping on my seat belt, smoothing down my skirt, finishing my latte. Ignoring him as best I could.

"Don't what?"

"Lie."

I looked out the window, away from him. Wishing he wasn't watching me so carefully so I could press my cold hands to my hot face. How was I going to sit here for the next seven hours and not fall to pieces?

"You think I'm lying?"

"I think you're made of lies, Gunnar."

"That summer..."

"I need to work," I interrupted, completely uninterested in rehashing that summer, and pulled my own work from my briefcase. All I had to do was get him home, and then I would leave and Gunnar would go back to being a regret and a slightly shameful hot memory that visited me in the darkest parts of the night.

The plane accelerated, lifting off into the starry sky. Taking us both home.

"Do you think I was lying that summer?"

"I don't want to talk about it."

"I think we need to talk about it if we're going to be working together."

Still not looking up at him, I laughed and laughed. "You're delusional if you think we're going to be working together."

"Brenna," he said, and when I didn't respond he unbuckled his seat belt and finally I looked up, startled, to find him moving from across the aisle to the seat right beside me.

"What are you doing?" I asked, reeling back as his knees touched mine and I couldn't avoid him. He was too tall. Too big. Too *there.*

"Trying to talk to you?"

"I don't want to talk," I said and picked up my report. The words I read were total gibberish.

And then he snatched the report out of my hand and tossed it onto the chair he'd just vacated.

I scowled at him and his silver-gray eyes walked over me. All over me. And I felt myself blushing. I felt the touch of my clothes on my skin, the movement of air in the jet. All of it.

He made me so fucking aware. Usually I lived deep inside my body. Hidden, half in my brain. But he pulled me out like some kind of reluctant sex snail.

"As your king, I command it."

"You're not my king yet, Gunnar."

"Formalities." He leaned back in his chair, stretching his legs out alongside mine, the fabric of his pants ghosting over my skin, and I flinched back so hard, I accidentally kicked my own chair.

"Is it so awful?" he asked, his face unreadable. And it was his cool and calm that made me feel so foolish. So out of control. "Being near me?"

You demolished me, I thought. *You wrecked me and it's taking all my strength just to pretend it didn't happen.*

"I don't care about being near you," I said, and he shook his head at me.

"Now who is lying?" he asked in a quiet tone.

We hit a bump of turbulence and I grabbed my latte cup in time, but the plane shook and then banked slightly.

"We have nothing to talk about," I said.

He reached out and grabbed my hand and it was electrifying. I actually gasped. Part horror. Part desire. He smiled at the sound I made and it was the smile he used to give me in my bed. In the cocoon we'd made. The smile that I'd foolishly thought for a few months meant something that it didn't.

Meant he cared.

I tried to yank my hand away but he held on hard. My fingers were crushed in his hand.

"You're hurting me," I breathed.

"Am I?" he asked blandly, and he loosened his grip but didn't let go of me. His fingers, instead of gripping mine, held mine. Slid between mine so we sat there with our hands clasped like lovers. "I never wanted to hurt you," he said.

I didn't struggle to get my hand free because he was stronger than me and I didn't know what he was after. So I left my hand limp in his. I would give him nothing. Not even my fight.

"Do you believe that?" he asked.

"No."

"You think I kissed you that day on the boat—"

"It doesn't matter. None of it matters."

"It matters to me," he said.

"Bullshit." I shook my head at him. "You left. You can't claim to care now."

"I didn't have a choice," he said. "You know that."

I told myself not to say it, to seal my lips against the words, to make my heart indifferent to the questions I wanted to ask. But I couldn't. In the end I'd spent three years asking exactly the same question, the only answer a silence that cracked pieces off me.

I drained my glass. Because if I was going to break something, I was really going to break it.

"You knew your father had a stroke," I said.

"The day after I left."

"And you didn't care?"

"About him? No."

"About us! The rest of us!" *Me!* "The rest of us you left behind."

His brow furrowed and he ducked down even closer to me. "Is that what you've been telling yourself? That I didn't care?"

"No. Asshole. You told us that. With your absence. With your fucking...vodka."

"The vodka is really bothering you."

"I don't give a shit about your vodka."

"Well, baby, you care about something." He was mocking me, his gray eyes sweeping over me, taking in my blush and my breasts and the breath I couldn't control.

"You," I said as clearly as I could. "Repulse me."

He tipped his head back and laughed. He laughed so hard he howled and I undid my seat belt and got to my feet. I towered over him, like this. And I loved it.

I tugged my hand, but he didn't let go. He stopped laughing and his silence was a powerful magnet, and as hard as I tried, I couldn't resist looking at him, only to find him staring at me. His eyes burning through the distance. Through my clothes. Through the years.

And suddenly it was as if we were *us* again. The two of us on that bed. In the library. All alone. Building a future I'd believed in with all my heart.

I could not tell if it was me holding his hand now. Or his holding mine.

"I was banished, Brenna."

"You could have found a way if you wanted to."

"Oh, Brenna. If only that were true."

"You know, fuck off. You don't get to rewrite what happened."

"What story have you been telling yourself all these years, princess?" he asked in a voice that turned my heart to liquid.

"No story," I said. "No story at all. Only the truth."

"Shall I tell you the story I told myself?"

"I don't care."

"I told myself I dreamed you. I dreamed every minute of the time I spent in your bed."

I jerked my hand free and stepped away from him. From the power of those words I did not want to believe.

"I'm never going to believe a word you say ever again," I told him, and I went to the back of the plane. And he had the good sense to stay away from me.

NOW
Gunnar

To be clear, I hadn't expected anything from her. I'd expected, actually, that she would leave after I left. I kept waiting for my phone to ring and for Alex to tell me that she'd gone. Left Vasgar and my father's machinations and gone on to find the life she deserved.

How stupid that was. I see that. How shortsighted. How conceited of me to have thought I knew what was best for her. She never took the easy way out of anything. If there was a fight, she was going to be in it.

Which made her walking away from me to sit in the

back of the jet more alarming. She wasn't even going to fight with me. I'd never expected her to smile and forgive me.

But I'd expected her to *fight*.

Three years was a long time to harden a heart. And hers was hard as stone.

After the longest flight in history, the jet touched down at Vasgar Airport and I felt a knot in my chest loosen, the muscles that had been clenched in my jaw relax.

Home. I was...home. Funny how much I'd missed it. Well, not funny really. Banishment had been harder than I'd expected. New York a strange island, so different from the one I knew. And every day that I'd gotten more used to the pace and the cement mountains of Manhattan, the more I'd wanted my homeland.

The people I'd met and spent time with were never the people I wanted. I'd missed Alec and Ingrid.

I'd missed Brenna.

I'd missed the smell of fresh snow and ice. The crooked streets and hidey-hole bars of my capital. The sheep and the fishermen. Spiced rolls. The whistle of the wind around the castle. I'd missed the stone walls and the cavernous fireplaces. I'd missed the library and the team I'd been a part of. I'd missed working toward change. Toward something better.

Home and Brenna. All of it.

I'd missed it all so much.

"Gunnar?" I glanced up to find Brenna standing there, her hat and coat on, ready to leave. Her face revealed her concern for a moment before she iced it over. "You all right?"

"I am," I said with a smile, blinking back the tears burning in my eyes. I stood and took my coat from the attendant. I smiled at her and smiled at Brenna.

"You don't seem all right," Brenna said.

That brief flash of concern gave me a sign of life. It showed me a chink in her armor. She was not as impervious as she wanted to believe she was, and I could work with that. I had won her over once. I could do it again.

"I'm home, Brenna. Everything is going to be fine."

NOW
Brenna

I WAS NOT interested in being moved by Gunnar. By his reaction to being home. Tears? I mean...come on. I call bullshit. But as the palace came into view through the windows of the limo we shared, I heard his breath hitch.

"I'd forgotten," he murmured, "how pretty it is at night."

He glanced back at me, one of his rare earnest smiles on his face.

I said nothing, refusing to share in his joy. Even though...yes...I thought that palace was always particularly beautiful at night.

"We'll need to set up a meeting tomorrow," he said.

"Alec will be able to help you with that."

"You've been running the country, Brenna. You don't think we should have a meeting?"

"I'm busy tomorrow."

"Okay, the next—"

"I won't work for you, Gunnar."

"With me. By my side—"

The car pulled to a stop and I got out.

"Jesus, Brenna...wait."

I turned and found him watching me over the top of the

car. The side doors to the throne room were open and I remembered painfully how he'd waited for me there when I came home from school. Because he wanted to see me before anyone else.

Real? I wondered. Or false?

Why...why would he do that if he didn't care? How elaborate a game could he have been building?

And then I remembered it didn't matter.

"I'll be at the funeral, the day after tomorrow," I told him. "Alec has been fully briefed."

"What happens after the funeral?" he asked.

I slammed the door shut and walked around the car, heading for the lights of the throne room.

"Brenna?"

He stopped me with a hand on my elbow. "Tell me," he said in a soft, slow voice. "Tell me what happens after the funeral."

"I'm leaving," I said, directly into his face so he'd hear me. Couldn't possibly misunderstand me. I shook off his hand and climbed the steps into the throne room, feeling him at my back the whole way. This was why I couldn't linger in the castle. I had to leave and leave fast. Because my entire body was alive around him.

Once we were inside, the guards shut the doors behind us and a page stepped forward from the thrones. Russell, one of the new interns from the high school program Alec had started.

There was no fanfare, no adoring public, because I wasn't sure I could actually bring him home. We'd save the parades for another day.

"Your Majesty," Russell said with his shy smile. "Welcome—"

"Leave us," Gunnar said.

Russell looked at me, the fear that he'd done something wrong settling over his face.

"Gunnar," I said. "This is—"

"I am your king," Gunnar said. "Please leave us. And shut the door behind you."

"It's fine," I told Russell. "Thank you."

Russell bowed his head and stepped backwards out the door. It shut behind him with heavy sound that echoed through the throne room.

"You can't just order people around," I said, feeling my heart beat in my throat. "Your father did that and no one respected him. You'll have to—"

"I left so you'd leave," he said.

"What?"

"I chose not to marry you so you could leave. So you could go to New York and be the person you should be."

There were a thousand things I couldn't make sense of. My brain was buzzing, my heart riding in my throat like fishing bobber.

"You...you don't get to decide that," I breathed. "Who I am. Or what I do."

"Clearly," he scoffed, the sound so familiar it actually hurt.

"Why?" I asked.

"Because the throne of Vasgar would have limited you. It would have been a stone around your neck."

"That's...that's why you told me I wasn't meant for the throne?"

He nodded, his eyes, his face, everything about him earnest in a way I wanted so badly to believe. "It's why I wouldn't marry you. Because part of my father and uncle winning means you lose. And there was no scenario where I could bear to see you lose anything."

Except you. I tried to pull my hand away but again he wouldn't let me.

"Do you believe me?" he asked.

"It doesn't matter if I believe you or not."

"It matters to me."

"No!" I cried. "You don't get to do this. You don't get to change everything three years later. You wrecked me, Gunnar. You destroyed me. I love—" I cut myself off ruthlessly.

"I loved you, too," he said, and it was my limit.

"Let me go," I demanded looking over his shoulder.

"I remember when I met you the first time. We were here in the throne room. It was so hot, remember?"

I shook my head, but of course I remembered. Of course every second with him was burned in my brain.

"And I thought that you looked like summer in Vasgar. You were so beautiful and fresh and...you did not care what we thought of you."

Right. That stunt with the book.

"I knew that day that you would change everything."

He stepped close to me. My hand still in his, I put my other hand against his chest, as if to push him away. But when I touched his body he exhaled a long, shaky breath. As if he'd been holding it.

And I did the same thing. The warmth of his body under my hand melted something and I wasn't pushing him away. I didn't have the strength to.

"I have thought of you every day," he said.

"Shut up. Shut—"

"Dreamed about you every night."

I kissed him. I kissed him instead of listening to him say things I couldn't believe.

For one breathless moment it was just my lips against

his. We didn't move. We didn't breathe. The earth turned beneath us. And then my better sense kicked in and I pulled back. Dropped my hand.

"Let me go," I said.

"I can't."

"Gunnar."

"I let you go once and it was the worst thing I've ever done. The biggest mistake I've ever made. I've spent years planning what I would do if I had you back in my arms."

My body went slack. My brain, however, buzzed into overdrive.

Don't. Don't believe him. Don't trust this. Don't let him back in.

"Let me show you," he breathed. Leaning forward. "I won't hurt you."

"You can't," I said with total bravado. A lie, really. I was building a fortress of lies to hide behind because my body was going to overrule my brain. My body always did when Gunnar was involved. "You can't hurt me. For you to be able to hurt me I would have to care about you. And I don't."

The door to the throne room scraped open. And Alec poked his head in.

"Gunnar!" he cried, breaking right through all the tension. Gunnar dropped my hand and I spun away from the two men, composing myself as much as I could. And then, while they hugged and slapped each other's backs, I walked right out of the throne room.

Two days. I only had to make it through the next two days.

CHAPTER 23

Now
Gunnar

THINGS MOVED QUICKLY after I got home. The next day was occupied with meeting the council. Foreign ministers. Finance minister. There were phone calls from dignitaries and interview requests from newspapers and media outlets around the world.

And Brenna was absent from all of it.

Her assistant, Gabriel, and Alec were guiding me expertly through most things, but the day stretched on and all I was aware of was Brenna's absence.

"Where is she?" I asked, putting the papers I was mostly not reading on my father's desk. I was using his office—my office now, I supposed, as my base. I needed Ingrid to come home and erase every impression of my father.

"Who?" Alec asked, sitting on the end of the couch in front of the fire. He had literally a mountain of reports for me to go through. Every piece of paper produced by Brenna and the council for the last three years.

"Brenna."

"Avoiding you. I think."

I pushed the intercom on the corner of my desk and that young kid I'd yelled at last night opened the office door.

"Your Majesty?"

"Russell," I said. "Have I apologized—"

"You have, sir. Several times."

"One more time then?" I asked, smiling at the kid. It was a joke now, between us.

"Go for it, Your Majesty."

"I'm sorry I was a monstrous dink."

"Apology accepted."

"Great. Do you know where Brenna is?"

"The library, I imagine." Russell looked over at Alec who was shaking his head, trying to tell the kid not to tell me, I suppose.

"Whose side are you on?" I asked my oldest friend.

"The side of peace," he said.

"Do I need to remind you that I saved your life?"

"Do you want me to go get her, sir?" Russell asked and I shook my head.

"Go back to doing whatever it is you do behind that closed door," I told Russell and the door clicked shut behind him.

I glared at Alec as I got to my feet.

"It hasn't been easy for her," Alec said.

"I know," I said. But Alec stood, too. It had been a long time since we'd fought. And I never won when we did. But if he wanted to go—

"You don't," Alec said. "We worked together every day. Ingrid was back and forth as much as she could be. Her cousin came home a few times and all of us talked about how...alone she was. She didn't let anyone close."

I did that.

"I'll make it right," I said.

Alec blew out a long breath. "Good luck, man. But I'm warning you. You hurt her again and I will come for you."

"Fair enough," I said and walked out of the old office and made my way across the castle to the library. Where there was a roaring fire and the smell of coffee and spiced rolls. And Brenna.

She was, of course, in her old spot at the table. Wearing a sweatshirt and leggings. Her braids had been tidied up.

When she saw me walk in she hit a button on her laptop and the sound of a crowd laughing was cut off.

"What do you want?" she asked.

I lifted my hands as if to show her I had no weapons. "To see you. What are you doing?"

"Watching clips of James McAvoy on the *Graham Norton Show*."

Not expecting her honesty, I laughed. "Alec and I are in meetings all day."

"Welcome home," she said with some irony. "Ready to run back to New York?"

"No." I pulled out one of the chairs and sat down, watching her stiffen as I did it. We'd been all kinds of awkward together over the years. But only because we hadn't known what to do with our feelings for each other. So we'd scrapped and bristled. We'd bared our teeth in smiles we didn't mean. But this...this chilly distance was new. And awful. I knew what would thaw it, of course. But there was no way to get from where we were now to fucking each other against the goddamned wall. At least, no way that I could see immediately.

"You know what I learned today?"

"Our fisheries are still in trouble."

"Well, yes. But you know what else?"

She shook her head.

"You were a very good leader, Brenna."

She swallowed, brushed some imaginary lint off her computer screen.

"It's in every report. And in every person I talk to. You are loved here."

"Well, after Frederick—"

"Don't. Don't sell yourself short. You did what no one else could have done."

"You could have."

No lie—the vote of confidence felt good.

"Stay," I said. "For the good of Vasgar. You and I...we don't even have to see each other."

She was shaking her head, just as I knew she would.

"I'm leaving the day after the funeral. I've wrapped up everything I was working on. Written all the reports. There are literally no loose ends—"

"I got a call from Donal McDonald. The investor would like to meet you."

She sat back in her chair. "Now? It's been two years."

I shrugged.

"He doesn't want to meet *you*?"

"Not according to Donal."

"Why didn't Donal contact me directly?"

"We were talking and he brought it up. He doesn't know we're..." I waved my hand between us. "Like this."

Strangers. So formal I was amazed our words didn't draw blood.

"Well, I suppose I can meet him in Inverness—"

"He'll be at the funeral."

"The investor or Donal?"

"Both."

She nodded. "Fine. I'll let him know—"

"I can do it," I said and stood. "I'll let you get back to your clips."

It wasn't fucking each other against the wall, but it bought me some more time.

NOW

Brenna

THE DAY of the funeral was dreary. Spitting rain and a vicious wind that made being outside a total misery. We wore black and bowed our heads, but I wondered if anyone standing at that graveside was actually going to mourn the man.

Not me. Or my mother, who pretended to wipe her eyes. Or Eric, who walked down the aisle of the church with an insolent swagger.

Gunnar seemed poised and stoic. Serious. Regal, even. The bad-boy prince was nowhere to be seen. He took my mother's arm and walked beside me like a leader.

A king.

Like the man I'd thought I knew. And I felt all my defences quake.

"Are you all right?" he asked me at the gravesite and I blinked up at him. He had raindrops in his hair. It beaded on the black cashmere of his coat. I brushed some off with my gloved hand.

"I'm fine. You?"

He glanced at the casket. The hole in the ground. The

crowds of people behind us. "Fine," he said. But he was lying.

The funeral had been televised. The interment had not been, but everyone at the funeral made their way to that hilltop cemetery to see Frederick laid to rest. Then we went back to the castle for a private lunch.

I expected the flask of akvavit to make an appearance. But Gunnar stayed sober. He had a whispered conversation with his uncle, who stormed out at the end of it, taking much of the tension in the room with him.

Everyone seemed to breathe a little bit easier once he was gone.

Everyone except Gunnar, who stood by the fireplace in the throne room. His back, tall and wide, to the room.

It was stupid to go over there and talk to him. I knew that and I managed to resist the urge for quite an admirable amount of time.

I found Donal shrugging into his coat near the doorway. "Donal!" I said with a smile, because I always enjoyed seeing him. He was a short man with thick glasses and was covered in freckles. He was too smart and too kind not to love.

"Hello, Brenna," he said and kissed my cheeks.

"I'm sorry I didn't get a chance to talk with you sooner," I said.

"Understandable. It was a busy day."

"Is the donor here?" I asked, looking around what was left of the crowd like I could pick him or her out.

"Ah...no," Donal said, wrapping his scarf around his neck.

"Was there a problem with his travel?" I asked. "Will be here tomorrow? I can meet him—"

"He will be here tomorrow," Donal said. "He looks forward to meeting you."

"This whole thing seems a little weird, doesn't it? I'm not in charge of anything anymore."

Donal smiled at me, the fire reflected in his glasses. "It's only a matter of time before you're in charge of something else. Of that I have no doubt. And if you are looking for employment, The MacDonald Group could always use someone with your talents."

"Thank you, Donal. I may take you up on that."

"I wish you would."

He squeezed my hand and left the throne room.

My mother had gone up to her rooms not long after the argument between Gunnar and Eric. The council members were thinning out, too. Gunnar was still there. Standing by the fire. I watched as a few members of council approached him and said their goodbyes. Watching him, he seemed so... lonely. Smiling and shaking hands, but encased in a sadness and a reserve that I'd never expected from him.

I was leaving tomorrow, after the meeting with Donal and the donor.

This was my last night in the palace.

My last night with Gunnar.

"Hey," I said, coming up to his elbow. For a second I had considered making a plate for him. The smoked salmon was delicious and the crab cakes, as well. Both things he loved. But I wasn't his mother. Or lover. And I didn't bring men food.

A smile ghosted over his face. "Brenna." That was all. Just my name.

"You okay?"

He nodded.

"Why do I think you're lying?"

His gray eyes slid over to me, widening slightly as if surprised. He glanced around the room and then back at me. "I guess I'm surprised by how...sad I am. He was not a good father. And I can't say with any confidence that he loved me or that I loved him. But he was my father and... well, the only parent I had left."

"It would be surprising if you weren't sad," I said, and his smile was a little warmer this time. "What happened with your uncle?"

Gunnar swore under his breath. "The bastard was using my father's funeral to try and drum up more support for his claim to the throne."

I gaped and then, because I couldn't help it, I laughed. "Ballsy."

"My uncle only has balls. Balls for brains."

I laughed again, and then he smiled and actually started laughing a little too. "So," I said, into this new easy space between us. "What did you tell him?"

"To leave."

"The funeral?"

"The country."

"You banished your uncle?"

"Nothing as dramatic as that, and frankly, after the last three years, the first thing I'm going to do is change the king's ability to banish people for any reason."

"It didn't seem so bad," I said, thinking of those ads and the clubs. The women. The damn vodka.

"It was hell, Brenna. Waking up every day and not being able to go home, to be with the people you wanted to be near. When I heard you'd stayed after Dad's stroke, I almost came back."

"That's crazy. You were banished, Gunnar. If you'd come back—"

"I would have been put to death. I know. Though, really, that seemed like a stretch. Alec convinced me, anyway, that I would only cause you more trouble. And the last thing I wanted was to cause you trouble."

I looked away, into the fire.

"During the funeral," he said, "I remembered being a kid. Still young enough to want something from my father that I didn't understand he didn't have in him to give. And as cold as my father was, my uncle was warm. He was boisterous and funny. He hugged me. The only person in my family who did." It was his turn to look into the flames and I stared at him. "And when he came to the castle, he always played games with me. Little things. Guessing which hand he had candy in, that kind of thing."

"It's hard to imagine," I said.

"Now, I know. But I don't think he was after the throne then. I think he was happy to let Dad run things."

"When did it change?"

"When does anything change? Slowly. Over time." He shook his head and laughed. "I'm sorry. You're on your way out the door. You don't care about this."

Oh, my god, I cared so much. I cared so much about that little boy, so hungry for attention he took scraps from an uncle who would end up betraying him. I cared so much about the man saying goodbye to his father and his uncle on the same day.

So much. Too much.

And I had one foot out the door. I did. I was leaving and I wasn't going to come back. It was the only reason I was contemplating the ridiculous thing I was contemplating.

Over the next few hours the fires died and the crowd thinned. Even Alec and Ingrid said their goodbyes. And I found reasons to linger until finally it was just Gunnar and me in the throne room.

"I'm...I'm going to go to bed," I said.

"Me, too." He nodded. "It's been a long day."

He said good-night to each of the servants and pages by name, and I felt something like pride lodge in my throat. Side by side we walked down the old stone hallways. I missed the first turn on purpose and he laughed.

"If there's a ribbon around your doorknob..."

"Oh, there is," I said. I didn't get lost anymore, but I liked the ribbon.

"I wish you would reconsider staying for the coronation," he said.

"I can't," I breathed.

Finally we stood outside my door and I felt this foolishness in my throat. My whole body was full of it. And when I turned to face him, I found him watching me. I found him...seeing me.

He took a deep breath, his eyes wide.

Please, I thought. *Please know what I need and don't make me say it. Please don't make me say it.*

"Brenna," he sighed. That was all, just my name.

His hand came up to my hair, touching my braids. His thumb brushed the outer curve of my ear, making my nipple hard in a wild, prickling rush.

"If you tell me to stop," he said, the smell of him washing over me in a way I used to love, "I'll stop. I will. But you have to say it. You have to tell me you don't want this."

His fingers trailed down the side of my neck, gooseflesh rippling up from his touch. My brain shorted out and it was just my body standing here. Skin and bones and a heart beating too fast, lungs breathing too hard.

"You remember what it was like between us," he asked. "How we couldn't get enough?"

"I..." My voice rattled off his fingers burrowing into my hair to grip the back of my neck. I knew what happened next. The way this whole story unfolded. I didn't want to remember.

But it was impossible not to.

"Brenna?"

"I remember."

His kiss was familiar. As familiar to me as breathing. He tasted of coffee and akvavit and him. His tongue stroked mine and I let him in. I gasped and moaned and I curled at the edges. All my steel beams and guard walls crumbled under the familiarity of his touch.

I knew, in my heart of hearts, that I'd missed it. That I'd craved it and longed for it.

For him.

But I had thought myself stronger than this.

"Yes or no, Brenna?" he whispered against me, his hand dropping mine to slide around my waist, pulling me into his body.

Yes and no, I thought. Yes, to this. To feeling this once more, and no to the rest of it. We had tonight before he would be swept up into being king.

And I would sweep myself away.

One night.

"Yes," I said.

CHAPTER 24

N OW
Brenna

HE GROWLED, low and dark, and my blood pumped harder and hotter through my body.

And I growled too, maybe.

I opened my door and we practically fell into my dark bedroom. The servants had lit the fire and it crackled, sending shadows dancing across the walls.

I pulled at his shirt so I could slip my hands up beneath the cotton to feel the heat of his body, the smooth satin of his skin.

He pulled at my shell. The silk was damp and wrinkled, and an instinct I had not expected kicked in and I put my hand against his. Stopping him.

"What?" he asked, leaning back, his lips swollen with the force of our kissing.

With the force of us.

That photograph and that horrible headline sat squarely in the middle of this moment. Three years old but suddenly so fresh it hurt. If you'd asked me a minute ago I would have said that I hadn't thought of that photograph or headline in three years.

"This isn't what I think it is, is it?"

I started to pull away but he wouldn't let me. His hand was on my hip. "Take off your shirt," he said, his voice cold. His eyes hot. A combination that had tied me in knots years ago.

"You know something, forget it. Forget this."

I started to step away but his body crowded mine.

"I've said no."

"No, you haven't," he said. "You've said a lot of things, but none of them have been no. You've said you don't like me and you don't respect me. You've said I'm beneath you and that's all very true. You are miles out of my reach, princess, you always were. But you have not said no."

He stepped closer again until his body was flush with mine and I felt his erection against my belly, and I tried, with little success, not to notice. But it was impossible. His desire was a bucket of kerosene over mine.

Was there anything more attractive than being desired by a person you desired? Even when it seemed unlikely, or born of false pretenses, I'd known he'd wanted me. I'd known that, against the odds, he desired me.

"And now I think something is bothering you and you aren't telling me what it is."

I shook my head. Doubt was a terrible houseguest.

"Do you know how long it took me to get you into my bed?" he asked.

"An afternoon," I said with a laugh.

"One year."

"Gunnar," I sighed. "Please, no lies."

"This isn't a lie."

"The first Christmas you came home from school. I met you in the throne room..."

"Yes. We fought like dogs the whole two weeks."

"You fought," he said. "You fought. You got off the plane with your teeth bared."

I had picked the fights. To try to protect our friendship. To try and protect myself.

"Perhaps," I said.

"You're right. I was never fair to you. I could never say the right thing. And I have a lot to make up for, but you walked into the side room in that red scarf, your eyes bright, your hair twisted in a bun on your head, and I realized what I had missed while you were gone."

"A chew toy?"

"You. You humming in the halls of the castle. You pushing me to be better, and if that didn't work, just plain shaming me into doing better. I missed the sound of your laughter and the way you got to the breakfast room first and took the parts of the newspaper you wanted before anyone else got there. I'd missed you, and when you walked in it was like I got a piece of myself back. I feel the same way right now."

I didn't know how to feel about what he said. About that winter years ago. About missing me like he missed a piece of himself. I didn't know how to feel about any of it and I took huge comfort in the fact that I didn't have to feel anything, really. Not at all.

Because I was leaving. Because this was goodbye.

"If this is about hiding," he said, "I'm not interested in that. Because you're fucking gorgeous. You are the sexiest, most exciting woman I've ever seen in my life. Every time you let me touch you I know how fucking lucky I am, and you have never believed that."

"I...I believed that you believed it."

Now he wasn't following me. He was stalking me. I stepped backward and he followed. Raw-boned and big, elegant, but wild beneath it all. My heart recognized him as someone like me, not just because we were from the same small place on the wildest edge of the world—but because we loved that place.

We fit that place.

His hand was suddenly at my lower back and he was still walking and I had no choice but to stay one step in front of him. Perhaps that was always my challenge with him. Staying one step in front of him. Planning just a little bit more. Wanting...just a little bit more.

My breath hitched and my heart pounded and all of a sudden the backs of my legs hit my bed. I sat down with a whoosh.

"What?"

He pushed me back and then, to my utter fucking delight, he got to his knees in front of me. His body pushing my legs out wide, as far as my skirt would allow.

My breath hitched, the memories burning me up from the inside.

"Remember this?" he asked, his eyes glinting like steel.

His hands slipped up under my skirt, reaching, I imagined, for the tops of my nylons, but he didn't find that. Instead it was the stretchy lace of a garter belt, the clips holding up the silk of my hose. And beneath that, the ruffled edge of my panties.

Had I worn this thinking of him? Maybe.

Probably.

The one-step-ahead thing. And maybe I'd just needed

the armor of all my beautiful things. My sexy things. My hair and the garter belt, the bra I was wearing.

They made me feel powerful.

But suddenly I realized, watching him bow his head in front of me like a supplicant at the ancient sites, that his reaction to all of this elevated it. My desire. My strength. My sense of power.

I felt good on my own.

He made me feel like a queen.

"Lift your skirt," he said, pushing the fabric up even as he said it. "Show me, Brenna."

He pushed, I pulled, and suddenly I was bared to him in the secret lace and satin I wore. For myself, yes.

And maybe for him.

Maybe because despite everything I'd known this moment would come.

And then, as I remembered he used to do, he leaned forward and kissed me through my underwear. A long kiss that would have been innocent if it weren't my pussy he was kissing. His hands stroked my thighs, strong and pale above the edge of lace.

"You're so beautiful," he said against me, the heat of his breath making me wet.

All of this was familiar, and yet not. Not really. Not totally. There was always the core of him that I didn't know. Couldn't trust. That made this feel unpredictable and dangerous.

I pushed my fingers through his thick dark hair, touching him as much as I could for as long as it lasted.

One night.

He licked me through the satin and I moaned, arching up into him, and he pushed his hands under my ass, holding me in place. His open mouth breathed hot air against me and I squirmed between his hands and his mouth.

"Yes," I moaned. My fingers in his hair pushed him just a little, just slightly, harder against me. I could feel him laugh; I could even feel him smile. And I remembered that, too. How much he liked my force. How exciting it had been that I knew what I wanted from him.

The same way I liked it when he threw me around the bed, lifting my legs and shifting my body until he had me where he wanted me.

"Like that," I said as he licked deeper into me through the satin. I knew he could taste me in the fabric and I knew —like an animal—he loved that. He loved all of that.

We had been—three years ago—really good animals together.

I shifted my hips, giving him room between my thighs, and within minutes he was pushing the underwear out of the way, his tongue hot and wet against me. He burrowed through me until he found the hard knot of my clit and he worried it with his tongue, stroked it and licked it until I was writhing against him. Panting and moaning his name. Asking for more. Asking for harder.

Suddenly he sat up, his face shiny, his eyes dark and focused. I swallowed audibly in the silence.

"I missed you," he said. And his words were arrows, sharp and sure right through my body. Lodging in the heart I'd tried to keep hidden.

"More," I said and pushed his head back down between my legs, and he laughed against me, but he found my clit again with his lips and his fingers left my ass to slide deep inside my pussy, filling me in a way I hadn't been filled in three long years.

I'd had sex since Gunnar. One time, just to prove to

myself he hadn't broken me. And then I'd buried myself in work.

But I could have fucked a million men and it wouldn't have mattered. There was no one like Gunnar.

He was—in this way, anyway—my very favorite animal.

The orgasm began twisting through me, building with every breath, every flick of his tongue, every sure and hard thrust of his fingers inside my body.

"Yes," I moaned, my voice breaking. I was clutching him to me at this point, grinding myself up into his face. "So good," I said, over and over again. "So good."

He sucked my clit into his mouth and I was done, bowing off the bed as I came and came and came and came.

And I was barely back in my body before he was standing me up, reaching under my skirt and tearing everything off me. The silk of the underwear, the stockings, the lace of the garter belt. All of it he tore off like they were ribbons under his hands. Strings.

He held me against him, one hand on my ass, the other sliding up between my legs again. I flinched, sore and twitchy.

And he gentled his touch, his mouth on mine. His breath in my lungs. His smell in my head. I reached between us and put my hand over his cock, stroking him through the fabric of his pants. He was long and hard, and I was instantly turned on again. Instantly poised on the edge of another orgasm.

I pulled my mouth from his, breathing hard, just like he was. Like we were running a race in this shadowed bedroom.

And I couldn't speak for him, but it felt like I was. A race against time. A race to gather up as many of these memories as I could for the years that were to come.

I was gathering a bouquet of orgasms to preserve—and I was just getting started.

"What do you want?" I asked him, and for a moment his eyes went wide, his mouth fell open, like he couldn't believe I would ask that.

And I felt myself retreat for just a second, pull away in the face of his surprise, but he grabbed my ass in his big wide palm and pressed my other hand against his cock through his pants.

"On your knees, Brenna."

Oh, that dark deep voice telling me to do dark deep things... I'd missed it. I'd missed it like a song I'd heard once and kept trying to remember.

I sat back down on the edge of the bed, my hand still stroking him through his pants, the other one holding on to his knee like I could keep him still for me.

I pushed harder against him until he hissed and I did it again. And then again. Until he finally pushed my hands away and unbuckled his belt.

"Do the rest," he said and the words weren't even out of his mouth before I had him unzipped, his pants pulled down, the dark cotton of his briefs yanked halfway down his legs.

His cock. God, his cock. He held it out to me.

"Lick me, Brenna."

I knew what he really wanted. Sure, he wanted my mouth, but what he really liked was watching me. He liked the sight of his cock disappearing into my face. And he really liked when I slipped one hand between my legs and stroked myself while I stroked him.

"Fuck," he gasped and groaned. "Yes. God. Yes. Just like that. So perfect. You were always so fucking perfect, Brenna. So fucking beautiful."

In this I felt pretty fucking perfect. Pretty fucking beautiful.

Powerful.

He cupped my head in his hands, careful of my braids, which made me smile. Or would have, if my lips hadn't been busy.

"Stop," he breathed. "Stop. Brenna. I'm going to—"

In the past, he'd pulled out. Come in his hand. Against my stomach. The bed sheets. I'd never swallowed and he'd never come inside my body. I didn't know how that had started. Him or me? No idea. But I was past such things now and I kept him there, in my mouth, my hand stroking him, my tongue licking him until he jerked against me. Roaring as he came in hot spurts into my mouth.

"Oh, my god," he gasped, pulling away from me to fall, sweaty and panting, onto the bed next to me. "Brenna..."

He left it at that and I wiped my mouth, smiling against my fingers. It was nice to surprise this man. Exciting, even. I opened my mouth to say something. To say anything, but he stood back up, and before I could stop him or say anything he'd lifted the silk shell I wore over my head.

"My god," he said. "You are so much more beautiful than I remembered."

His hand touched the curve of my breast, lifted in the wire and lace of my bra, cupped it in his palm. His other hand doing the same. I squeezed my thighs together, the orgasm building between my legs.

He pushed me back on the bed his big body coming down over me, and it was all that I remembered. Comforting, in a way, to be so covered by him, but thrilling, too. He kissed my breasts. The trembling curves, the nipples beneath scratchy lace.

Kissing was too tame a word. And I couldn't think of the

right word. My brain was being fried by his touch, my body rising to his attention like the sun over the side of the earth.

Inevitable.

"You've been with other people," he said. Not a question, but a comment. A thought said out loud.

"Yes."

"How many?"

"Why does it matter?"

The dark flop of his hair fell into his eyes as he looked up at me over my breasts. "Everything you do matters to me."

"Gunnar," I sighed, and he lifted himself up, bracing himself on his elbows beside me.

"Tell me."

"One. I was with one man, about a year after you left."

"Did you date? Were you together awhile?"

"No." I laughed. "I had my one and only one-night stand. Just to prove I could. Just to prove I wasn't broken."

"And?"

"What do you want me to say? It was amazing. I didn't think of you once. I didn't close my eyes, trying not to cry because all I wanted was you."

"I'm sorry."

"What about you, Gunnar? Are you going to regale me with tales of the women you've had in your bed?"

"Would you believe me if I said I hadn't been with anyone since I left you?"

"No. I saw you there, Gunnar. You were surrounded by women."

"None of them was you."

"Is this... Why are you doing this?"

"Because I don't know how to stop." His eyes swept over my body and his hand followed. My collarbone, to my breasts, over my thighs, under my skirt until his hand found me again. The wet, hot heart of me. I gasped as his finger slipped in. His eyes on mine, he breathed in and out, and with my eyes on his I did the same, like I couldn't do anything else but breathe and let him penetrate me.

"Spread your legs," he whispered and I shifted my skirt, lifting it up to my hips. He slid another finger inside of me, his eyes on mine, watching my face react to his penetration. To his having of me. "Wider," he said. And I did. Because I didn't know how to stop, either.

He had three fingers inside of me and I had to breathe through my mouth. I had to close my eyes because looking at him hurt. I had to concentrate on the feelings of sex, because the feelings of him were too much. Much too much.

"I haven't had sex with a woman since that morning in your bed. And I wanted to," he said. "I wanted to fuck you out of my system. Out of my head and out of my heart, but every time I started...every time I touched a woman, all I could think of was you. Look at me, Brenna," he said and again, so powerless, I opened my eyes.

"Am I lying?" he asked.

"I don't know," I breathed.

"Yes, you do," he said, slowly easing his fingers out of me only to push them back inside. I was slick and wet and I wanted him more than I wanted to talk. More than I wanted answers to these questions. But he seemed focused. He seemed to need me to believe him.

"No," I finally said. "You're not lying."

"I want you to come again," he said, and I nodded, gulping back air. His thumb found my clit and his hand worked me over like an instrument, and within minutes I was shaking and crying.

And then I was coming. I was coming all over his hand

and all over myself and I could feel how wet I was down over my ass and onto the quilt. Before I could be embarrassed or nervous or actually form one coherent thought about it, he pulled me up until I was standing on shaking legs, held up by his hand on my elbow.

"What?" I gasped, still trying to catch my breath. He pulled me to him for a long beautiful kiss. Sweet and rough all at once. Wild and restrained. It was everything, this kiss, and I fell against him with greed. Wanting more of this kind of kiss. Wanting nothing but this kind of kiss for the rest of my life.

I was so far from who I thought I was at this point, I didn't even recognize myself.

But why can't I be this person and a lawyer and a leader of state and...this man's lover? Maybe...maybe we could do that. Be lovers on the sly. Why not? We could be careful. Secretive.

God, how predictable, I thought. How disappointing I was. One orgasm and I was ready to give this man the best of myself. While expecting nothing in return.

This is why I had to leave.

He stood, taking off his clothes. Kicking off his shoes until he stood in front of me naked. The firelight cast him in gold and he'd never been so beautiful.

The tattoo across his chest made him seem so deadly. And the look on his face made him seem so royal.

"You're not naked," he said.

"I'm looking at you."

"I remember what you did the first time I took off my clothes," he said. "Do you?"

"Was it something embarrassing?"

"You closed your eyes. Wouldn't open them."

"Sounds about right."

From thin air, it seemed, he pulled out a condom.

Ripped it open and rolled it down over his dick, which I watched, breathless and achy.

"Do you remember what I did when I saw you naked?"

I nodded because it was one of my favorite memories.

"Say it, Brenna."

"You got down on your knees," I whispered. "And thanked all the old gods."

"For what?"

"For the privilege of being my lover."

"That's right," he said, his voice soft. "Take off your skirt and get on the bed, Brenna."

I did what he asked, wondering why I felt like crying. My skirt hit the floor and I kicked off my shoes before sitting on the bed, the fur on my bed soft against my thighs. He was right there, pushing me back, laying me down with his body.

And when the focus of his eyes got to be too much, I kissed him. I kissed him and kissed him. Putting all of this confusion and all of this pain into it. I kissed with my tongue and my teeth and all of my heart and he groaned against me, settling his body against mine. His weight pressed me deeper into the furs until I felt like I was surrounded by all things Vasgar.

Home, I thought, delirious with sex and love and grief. This felt like home.

And then I felt him between my legs, the brush of his knuckles against my clit and then him pushing inside of me. I felt my breath leave my body in one long ecstatic gasp.

I missed this. I missed this so much.

"Me, too," he said, and I realized I'd said it out loud. I'd told him that I missed this and all at once it didn't matter. He could know this and it didn't hurt me. Nothing could hurt me when I was so ecstatically full. Of him. Of us. Of what sex should be. Of what love felt like.

I could do this and say goodbye and my heart...oh, my heart would be okay.

Maybe not right away. But in time.

I wrapped my arms around his neck and I held him as close as I could.

Lifting my hips, I took him deep. And slowly he pulled out and then pushed back in and within seconds it wasn't enough. The long, slow fucking didn't keep pace with the frantic rhythm of my heart. And I could feel the tension in his body, too. How carefully he was holding on to something he really wanted to let go of.

"Fuck me," I breathed. "Like you used to."

And that, it seemed, was all it took. He held on to me, his fingers in my hair, his elbows squeezing my shoulders, and he thrust as hard as he could, so hard we moved across the bed, my head soon hitting the headboard. It was impossible to breathe or think or do anything but hold on and feel, and then he slipped a hand between our bodies and his thumb rode down hard on my clit and I shattered into a thousand pieces. I was stars in a dark sky. Scattered and random. Blinking with my own light.

And he followed right after me, groaning into my ear, curling himself up against me as he twitched and shook and fell to pieces. And I stroked his back, remembering the sweetness we used to have. Remembering when I used to love him.

How easy it had been, I thought.

Maybe that was the nature of lies. Once they were believed, they were nothing but sweet and satisfying. They were false food I could have lived on for days.

Gunnar kissed my shoulder. The side of my neck. Wet,

sloppy kisses that made no sense. And then he rolled away, flopping back on the bed. And I felt the chill come back. The silence. The lies and the things I wanted to believe despite knowing better.

I sat up, swinging my feet to the ground, wincing as my body recalibrated. I would be sore between my legs for days, a dirty reminder of a dirty man.

A dirty love.

I stood up, taking inventory as I walked over to the dresser. My hose were ruined. My shirt. From the drawers I grabbed a new pair of underwear, dark jeans. A sweater and a new bra. He was watching me from the bed. I could feel his eyes.

"You're still going to leave, aren't you?" he asked.

"Sex...doesn't change anything," I said.

"Funny."

He got up off the bed and I felt myself panic, all my calm shattering under the sudden heat of his temper. Of his focus. He pulled on his pants but didn't buckle them. The rest of his clothes he just gathered in his arms for the short walk down the hall to his room.

"What's...what's funny?" I asked.

"For me, sex with you changed everything."

CHAPTER 25

N OW
Brenna

I DIDN'T SLEEP. Not in the sheets that smelled like Gunnar. Like sex. I sat in the chair and stared into the fire and tried to imagine what my life was going to be like once I left Vasgar.

And I couldn't.

My imagination faltered just outside the door of the palace.

Or maybe it was my enthusiasm that faltered.

The alarm went off at 7 a.m. I slapped it off and went to shower and change for my last meeting in the castle.

Coffee on my empty stomach made me nauseous, so I showed up outside the king's office feeling not entirely myself. Sleepless and sick, it took me a second to recognize Donal sitting at the desk to the left of the shut door.

"Donal!" I said. "What are you doing out here? Are we the first ones?"

He shook his head. Signing his name to a paper he slipped into a manila envelope. He handed me the envelope. "You can go on in."

"What is this?"

"Gunnar will explain."

"Gunnar is in there?" I asked. "I thought I was meeting..."

My breath caught as some penny in the back of my mind finally dropped. American donor, my ass.

I pushed open the door to find Gunnar sitting alone in his office. He looked exactly right behind that big desk. He was proportional to the job sitting back there.

"It was you!" I yelled.

He nodded, a smile that did not at all come close to reaching his eyes. He seemed...dim...this morning. All his voltage turned down.

"Honestly, Brenna, I thought you would catch on by now."

"How did you do it?"

"Donal did most of it. He's the hero in the story. I just sold my soul for some vodka."

"The goddamned vodka!"

"Yes. The goddamned vodka."

He got up from behind his desk and held out his hand for the manila envelope I'd forgotten I had. I gave it to him. He opened the file and spread out the papers, signing his name where there were little red stickies.

"Are you dissolving the deal?" I asked. "Is that it...you're pulling the money?"

.   .   .

NOW

Gunnar

I HAD DONE TOO good a job making her believe I didn't love her. The lies I told trying to get her to leave the country had been too effective. And my silence the last three years had only cemented it.

I held out the pen for the woman I loved to take, but she didn't. She was staring at me with red-rimmed eyes, her hands in fists at her sides.

"I should have known the damage my lies would do," I told her. "I knew you too well, just like you knew me, and when I chose to hurt you instead of love you—I knew exactly what would hurt you the most."

Her eyes looked me over, like they always did when she walked into a room, and I wondered if she knew she did that. Like she was checking I had all my parts before she looked at or talked to anyone else.

I'd loved that three years ago, exploited it, maybe.

But I'd been a royal dick back then.

"I bought my first apartment building when I heard you got the job in New York City," I said. "I knew we couldn't be together, but I just...I wanted to help you. Be close to you."

"How did you have the money? I thought your dad disowned you."

"I'd saved it over the years. Bits and pieces. I'd thought, for a long time, before you came along, that I would leave Vasgar to my uncle. And I would live a life away from the throne."

"Well, I guess you still got to live your dream, huh?"

"About a month into the banishment, I realized that my

reputation, such as it was, had value. Real value. And...my looks didn't hurt."

"No, I don't suppose they did."

"The vodka company approached me and offered serious money for the use of my face and the...Wicked Prince of Vasgar reputation, and I said yes."

"And sent the money to me?"

I nodded.

"Did anyone else know?"

"Only Donal. I wanted to tell you, if only to redeem myself in your eyes. But I couldn't risk my uncle and father finding out."

Her sweet pink mouth fell open; her eyes went wide. "Oh, my god, even from New York you managed to stop what they were doing."

"When I found out you'd stayed, I wanted to tell you. I nearly called you a million times. I thought if you knew, you'd...see that you didn't need to sacrifice yourself to the work you were doing. You could leave."

"I chose to stay."

"I know, and Donal made it clear to me that if you knew I was the investor you still wouldn't leave. He reminded me of what I'd forgotten."

"What was that?"

Truthfully, I'd thought about what I would say to her in this situation about a dozen times. But all those speeches abandoned me. It was shameful how I'd thought I knew what was best for her. How I'd misjudged and hurt her.

"I kept remembering how happy you were leaving for Edinburgh. How your entire being lit up when you talked about working for the UN, living a life away from Vasgar. And I wanted you to be happy like that."

She looked away, out the window. Her throat bobbed as she swallowed.

"You love Vasgar. And you were happy those months before it all fell apart. The work you did—"

"I loved it."

"And I...I underestimated that. And your patriotism. And loyalty."

I nodded. "It was ridiculous of me to think that I knew what was best for you, but three years ago, I did. I thought I knew what was best, and I would have done anything for you to be free of the castle. I really did think you'd leave and I had this dream that you would be in New York and I'd...orchestrate some casual chance meeting with you. And we'd...we'd have a chance to start over. Without the throne. Without our parents. Just us." It sounded like a fairy tale. "But you stayed."

"I couldn't leave...the work we were doing..."

I nodded, my mistakes around me like blast sites. "I was stupid and blind and I should have seen that coming. I should have known that about you, that you would always do the job. That you would always do what was right. That I was the selfish one."

"Those things you said," she whispered. "That morning with our parents."

"I'll regret them until I die. And I'll regret that I did not protect you the way I should have."

She bit her lip and looked out the window.

"I want to give you what you want," I said, the words sticky in a mouth full of regret.

That made her look at me, her eyes wide.

"If you want to leave, I won't stand in your way. I owe you that. You can leave knowing I will fight for everything you have fought for the last three years. I'll live up to the challenges you've set for me."

"I know you will," she breathed, and that...god, that was a relief.

"Or I will put you on the council. My uncle's position at the head of the table. You can work for Vasgar from council chambers." I took a deep breath. "Or I will marry you and go back to New York and leave you to rule the country."

"Gunnar!" she gasped.

"Because you are the right person for that job. You always have been. And that I led you to believe for a moment that you weren't worthy of the throne is my greatest regret. It's the throne that isn't worthy of you."

"Is that...what is that?" she asked, pointing to the papers.

"Marriage contract. And another one promising that I'll leave and you can run the country with no interference from me."

She stepped up to the desk, touching each piece of paper with shaking fingers. Her fingertips brushing over my signature.

"Say it again," she whispered.

"We'll get married and I will live in New York—"

"No," she said. She lifted her head and her eyes; her beautiful blue eyes were full of tears. But her mouth, her mouth was lifted in the smallest smile. The most careful smile, as if she, too, was trying not to wish too much.

"I love you," she said in the ancient language.

And I said it back to her before the words were fully out of her mouth. I said it over and over again, until she put her fingers against my lips.

"I love you, too," she said. "I have...forever."

"What do you want?" I asked. "What can I give you?"

"Marry me," she said. "And let's rule Vasgar side by side."

I crushed her in my arms, my warrior princess. My Viking love. I hadn't been brave enough to dream of this, but here it was.

The dream of us had been too strong to be killed by my stupidity. My foolishness.

"Marry me," I said. "Marry me and rule beside me and I will spend every day of my life on my knees in front of you, thanking the old gods."

She laughed, kissing my face, the tears she'd been holding back sliding in silver tracks down her beautiful face.

"Good," she whispered. "Because that is what I want."

"My queen," I whispered into her hair. "You are and always will be my queen."

"King Gunnar," she whispered back. "Long live my wicked, wicked king."

EPILOGUE

N OW
Brenna

I HAD DÉJÀ VU. I was in a car approaching the ancient church at the far end of North Island. A white tent was set up on the green space between the palace and the church. Edda was there. So was Ingrid.

They were drunk on champagne. I was not. I was drunk on something else entirely.

Gunnar. Love. All of it. The whole fairy tale.

It was my wedding day.

My mother was involved only because she had to be. But Ingrid managed her like a champ and she impacted the beauty of my day not at all.

Neither did Gunnar's uncle, who'd been arrested a year ago for tax evasion.

This was a day for the kingdom and our friends.

And us. Mostly for us.

"You ready?" Ingrid asked as the car pulled to a stop in front of the church. The sky was endlessly blue beyond the stone steeples.

Ready? What a ridiculous question. I was beyond ready.

We'd waited three years after Frederick died. Slowly introducing the idea of us to the public, braced at every turn for disaster.

But it never came.

If our parents had been a fairy tale, we were something...steadier. More tangible. We were love, yes. So much love. But we were hard work and total honesty, too. We were good for each other and good for the country.

And we were embraced because of it.

Beloved.

"So ready," I said. My two maids of honor, both a little drunk on a special batch of Alec's akvavit, beamed at me.

"Okay, one more for the road," Edda said, lifting the flask to her bright red lips. My bridesmaids were in deep purple and carrying bunches of white calla lilies. I was in white carrying purple calla lilies. I couldn't image them or myself being more beautiful.

Ingrid put her hand on Edda's hand. "One more for the road is how he gets you."

"Who?"

"Alec."

"Well..." Edda twinkled. "If that beast of a man wants to get me—"

I coughed and shook my head. Ingrid and Alec were so on again, off again, it could make your head spin, but Ingrid put up her hand. "No," she said. "It's fine. We're done."

"I've heard that before."

"I'm just saying. The akvavit sneaks up on you," Ingrid said. "One more for the road is usually a bad idea."

Edda and I shared a look and Ingrid rolled her eyes. "Don't give me the fisherman's daughter from South Island stuff."

Edda and I laughed. "Okay," I said and kissed her cheek. "I won't. Now, come on. I want to get married."

Edda popped open the door and one of the ushers was there to open it the rest of the way and help each of us out of the car. There were hundreds of people standing outside the church. Citizens of Vasgar who just wanted to catch a glimpse of me and Gunnar. People who just wanted to be a part of the day.

I lifted my hand, my veil caught the wind and billowed out around me, and I could hear the shutter snaps of dozens of cameras. My dress was simple in its design but covered in lace and beads and sequins. And my veil was nearly as long as the train of the dress.

It was stunning and made me so happy, but it was a bit of a production.

Edda and Ingrid grabbed my train in their hands and together we made our way to the church. The doors opened and horns trumpeted my arrival. More ushers opened the door to the sanctuary and there, at the front of the church, was Gunnar.

He wore his black military uniform, the one that made my heart pound. The one that made me feel like I needed to be pinched, because surely this was a dream.

That man, the king, was my dream.

I pressed my fingers to my lips at the very same time he did, and laughing, we gave each other the same salute.

Respect and love. Forever.

My mother was seated in the front of the church, wearing a mother-of-the-bride dress with a black ribbon attached to the bodice in keeping with our country's widow tradition. She'd been pissed about that, but my mother being pissed didn't even register on the beauty of the day.

Alec stood beside Gunnar as his best man. His shock of red hair was already breaking free of whatever product he'd used to try and control it. He also wore his dress military uniform, but truly I only had eyes for Gunnar.

I walked down the aisle toward him on my own. My own person, giving myself to him under my own command. Just as he stood there, giving himself to me.

"You're beautiful," he whispered when I reached him. He took my hands in his and kissed them. "I'm so lucky, Brenna. I'm so lucky."

"We both are," I said. Together. The two of us. We'd forged our own path here and we'd make our own future. Together we turned to the priest and the windows that were letting the light of a brand-new day.

I HOPE you enjoyed My Wicked Prince! If you want more information on new releases, sales or exclusive freebies find me in any of these places:

Newsletter sign up: http://www.molly-okeefe.com/subscribe/

Bookbub: https://www.bookbub.com/authors/molly-o-keefe

O'Keefe's Keepers: https://www.facebook.com/groups/1657059327869189/

Want more heart-stopping, sexy romance? The King Family Saga is available now and free on KU. Enjoy this excerpt of THE TYCOON.

http://geni.us/Fnh2P

PROLOGUE

V ERONICA

No one had ever told me about orgasms.

Like, I had a sense, from movies or whatever. But no one ever gave me the complete picture. How they were tricky. How you had to be patient and vulnerable. Naked in a lot of ways—more than just, you know, actually naked. No one told me that they were a little frightening, that feeling of chugging up the incline of a roller coaster. Of something powerful and scary being just over the edge of a cliff.

Really, what no one told me was how freaking consuming they were.

After having some (eight, to be exact), it was literally all I could think about. Even in this stupid dress with the suffocating shapewear and the itchy netting. The boning in the bodice that dug into my armpits and didn't let me breathe.

The way my boobs—always a problem, except in the orgasm department—were squished and flattened.

All of this should be awful. But it wasn't. Not really.

Because it was my engagement party.

And all I could think about was sex.

And Clayton.

"You didn't lose the ten pounds you were supposed to, did you?" my stepmother, Jennifer, asked. She had her disapproving sniff going at full speed.

"Nope," I answered.

"Veronica," she said and then sighed, the most disappointed sigh. "You were going to try."

"Was I?"

Clearly, while I'd been thinking about sex, my stepmother had been thinking about the ten pounds she wanted me to lose. The urge to tell her to just calm down, was hard to resist, but I managed -- because orgasms. I used to obsess over those ten pounds, too, and all it got me was another five.

But this was what she'd done to my half-sister, Sabrina. She'd tried to bully and shame her into a size zero. The woman just couldn't stand to see a girl eat bread. Or be happy.

I would never understand how my father could go from my beautiful, loving mother to Jennifer. They were diametrically opposed.

"Tonight..." Jennifer said, straightening herself up so she looked like the stick that had been stuck up her ass. She wore a blue dress that hugged her body so closely I could practically see her hip bones through the material. "...is important."

I was twenty-two, not twelve. And it was my freaking night and no one needed to tell me what was important. I turned to face her instead of dodging her gaze in the mirror and I looked right at her. Something I never would have had the courage to do before the last few weeks with Clayton.

But I've had eight mind-bending orgasms—and they'd brought me some kind of new confidence I'd never had before.

"Jennifer," I said, right in her frowny face. "It's my engagement. It's my party. It's my body. And none of it concerns you."

Jennifer sniffed so hard she nearly turned herself inside out.

Behind me, Trudy swallowed a laugh. She'd been brought into the upstairs dressing room of The King's Land Ranch to literally sew me into my dress—no zippers for the girl who didn't lose the ten pounds.

"We're nearly done," Trudy said around the mouth full of pins between her lips. A few more tugs and twitches on my dress and she stood back and smiled at me. "*Eres bonita.*"

I believed my old friend when she said I was pretty, because for one of the few times in my life—I felt pretty. I felt it down in my bones. Tonight was going to be amazing.

"*Gracias.*"

Trudy helped me down from the dais where I'd been standing surrounded by mirrors. A thousand reflections of myself stared back at me. It wasn't pleasant.

"Do you know where my sister is?"

"Where do you think your sister is?" Trudy asked with a laugh, sticking the pins she'd had in her mouth into the pincushion she wore on her wrist.

I sighed. The stables. Probably in her dress, too.

"What have I said about speaking in Spanish, Veronica?" Jennifer asked.

"More than half the people who live on this ranch speak

Spanish," I said, shaking out the skirt of my sparkly tea-length gown. "You could try learning it. But if you don't want to hear it, you should move."

Jennifer stepped up to me so fast she was like a snake coming out of the bushes. And her face...uh-oh...I'd pissed her off.

I tried not to smile.

"I have spent the last sixteen years thinking this day would never come. That you would never find a man to get you out of this house. But it's here and I'm so glad you are leaving." She spat her venom all over the place. And once upon a time her words would have hurt, more than hurt, maybe. But Clayton and the orgasms were like armor. "You and your alcoholic sister need to just get out of my house."

"Bea's not an alcoholic," I said, but Jennifer was already leaving. "She's just fun!" I shouted at her back.

And then it was just me and Trudy in this stupid hall of mirrors.

Trudy touched my back, trying to be comforting, but if I had armor around myself, my weak spot was Beatrice. I would have left this house a long time ago if it hadn't meant leaving Beatrice here. Sabrina, too, for that matter.

Someone had to take care of them.

"Don't let her get to you. Tonight is too special," Trudy said.

Right. I was twenty-two. Sabrina a year out of high school. I could have this life. The orgasms and Clayton.

The whole fairy tale.

"You deserve to be happy." Trudy eyed me sideways, a smile on her face. She was married to Oscar, who ran my father's stables, and while not employed officially by the King family, she'd stepped in when my mom died and has always been really good to me and Bea. A motherly buffer between us and our stepmother.

We hugged and Trudy left to change her clothes. Her hair was already done, with the white mock-orange flowers from the shrubs behind the house tucked into her curls. I had the same in mine. Well, sort of. They were already slipping out. I turned in the mirror so I could try and tuck them back in, but it wasn't much help. My brown hair was so straight it was impossible to get things to stay. I was doing my best with the bobby pins, but I didn't have my glasses and my fingers looked like pink blurs in a bigger brown blur.

"Hello, Veronica."

Oh, God. A tide of heat rolled over my body and the bobby pin dropped from my suddenly numb fingers.

It was Clayton. And, just like that, I was breathless. Hot.

He stood in the doorway, a black blur that became clear as he walked toward me. My God, that man in a tux. It shouldn't be legal. He was handsome enough without the bespoke black coat and crisp white shirt, but with them he was nearly unbearable. His dark hair was swept back from his face. And I didn't know if you could call a face dangerous, but if you could, his was. His nose was maybe too big, his cheekbones too sharp. His resting face was utterly unreadable with perhaps a hint of disdain. His eyes were a penetrating dark brown. Nearly the color of his hair. But his lips. His lips were the rudest thing I'd ever seen. Thick and full. Slow, painfully slow, to smile.

And they tasted so good.

He looked like one of those intense Irish actors. Broody and dark. And the way he watched me; it was like he couldn't wait to take me apart with his teeth and put me back together with poetry.

He was the brightest thing I'd ever seen and I had to look away. Look away or go blind. Or go crazy. Or strip this damn dress off and ask him to do what he did to me in his office last week.

"Let me help you."

"With what?"

"The flower?" He crossed the dressing room and crouched at my feet. I stared up at the ceiling and prayed for strength. For calm.

Just...be cool, Ronnie.

He stood holding the mock-orange blossom in his fingers. The smell, thanks to my crushing of the delicate thing, filled the small space between us. It was heady. Like champagne on an empty stomach.

"Where does it go?" he asked.

"My hair...but I can't—"

"You're not wearing your glasses."

I used to think he never smiled. When I met him four years ago, he was humorless. Stern. None of the Irish poet, only the businessman Dad had hired to manage the amalgamation of some of his companies.

But in the last six months, as we started dating he smiled more.

And I knew that was because of me.

He brought me orgasms. I brought him smiles.

Not sure if it was fair, but it was real.

"Why aren't you wearing your glasses, Veronica?"

"They don't go with the dress."

He put his hands to my waist and I swallowed a moan low in my throat.

Kiss me, I thought. *Please, just kiss me. Let's not go downstairs. Let's not do this whole party. Let's shut the door and take off these clothes...*

He turned me until I faced the mirror and it was everything I could do not to close my eyes. I hadn't looked in the mirror while Trudy was sewing me into my dress, or earlier, when Sabrina was helping me with my makeup.

I didn't know myself in this moment, so instead I looked at Clayton.

I couldn't say I knew him any better, but he was so damn fun to look at.

"You're nervous?" he asked. His fingers found my bobby pin and tucked the flower back into the elaborate twist that was my hair.

"A little."

"Me, too."

I laughed. "I don't believe you."

"Why?" he asked. Our eyes met in the mirror and it was a strange, diffused connection. Painfully intimate.

"You don't seem nervous about anything. Ever."

Clayton projected a kind of detachment. An unruffled coolness. He was the picture of control. Except... I thought of that time in his office. And again in his condo. That last date when he'd cooked for me.

He hadn't been cool then. His hands had shaken when his fingers combed through my hair, when he held my skull in his palms. His voice had broken when he moaned, "So good, Veronica. You suck me so good."

Between my legs I suddenly throbbed.

"You're beautiful."

It was weird. Well, maybe not weird, but he always said I was beautiful. He never said I looked beautiful. Every compliment I'd ever gotten on my looks had been about the dress I was wearing or how I'd done my hair. The implication being that without adornment I was not beautiful.

But Clayton was not commenting on the fancy Oscar de

le Renta gown. Or my hair. Or the smoky eyes Sabrina had given me.

He was talking about me. Myself. My body. The skin I lived in.

It wasn't something you noticed until someone said it to you repeatedly. Especially a man like him. Not just that he was handsome or that he was sexy.

It was that he was never wrong.

"This dress," he whispered, and his fingertips brushed over the strapless bodice. Not quite touching my breasts but close enough that I knew he was doing it on purpose. "Is perfect for you."

He hummed low in his throat. And his hand ran from my breast down my waist to my hip. The dress was seven thousand layers of pink tulle with gold sparkles and crystals sewn into every layer. The bodice was fitted but the skirt flared out at my waist. Not poufy, just...forgiving.

It was a beautiful dress and I felt beautiful in it. Except that it was too tight.

"I have something for you," he said.

"Clayton," I sighed. "You don't have to give me anything."

The ring on my finger, the orgasms. The happiness I felt. All of it was enough. Except...well, he could tell me he loved me. That would be something. A gift.

Two months ago, after we'd had sex for the first time (after the first two of my orgasms), we were lying in the big king-size bed in his home, sweating into his sheets, and I'd blurted that I loved him. He'd kissed me, given me the third orgasm. And the next day he proposed.

Maybe he didn't love me. Maybe he just liked me a lot. Maybe he was pretty sure that he would love me at some point, and just wasn't there yet.

Or maybe...just maybe...he did love me, and he just didn't know how to crack through that armor he had around him.

I voted that option. Because there was no reason for him to do the things he did unless he felt something real for me. And because I didn't want it to be awkward, I hadn't told him I loved him again. Except a few times when he'd fallen asleep before me, the dark splash of his hair falling down on his forehead. Those rude-boy lips parted as he breathed.

At that moment I couldn't resist and the words slipped out in a whisper against the skin of his shoulder. Secrets I kept in the night.

Clayton pulled an oblong box out of the inside pocket of his tuxedo jacket and my stomach fluttered. He was so good at picking out jewelry for me. My engagement ring was an antique Tiffany-set sapphire. Elegant, with a bit of filigree around the impressive stone to make it unique. It was my favorite thing in the world.

He handed me the box with the half curl of his lips that made him seem so boyish. I wanted to hug him. Tousle his hair. Whisper *I love you* against the pulse in his neck.

"Open it," he said.

"You don't have to—"

"I know."

I opened the box and in it was a beautiful necklace. Antique. Victorian, maybe. A long gold chain with a diamond and pearl pendant. A giant diamond.

"I saw it and thought of you." He took it out of the box to put it around my neck where the chain and jewels glittered and gleamed in the lights and mirror. The touch of his fingers against my nape made my breath hitch.

"I have something for you, too," I said, and stepped away

from his touch over to where I had put my clothes. My jeans and Converse. My purse. I pulled out the box for him.

This might be a mistake. So dumb. I mean, the man had no need for something as old-fashioned as this. But...I saw it and thought of him. I held the box out.

He seemed weirdly flabbergasted. Like he didn't know what to do with the package I was offering him. Or maybe like he didn't want it. He looked at the box and then at me, his armor totally in place.

How, I wondered in the back of my brain, have I managed to get engaged to a man I can't read? Like, what kind of lunacy was that?

"You can open it later." Embarrassed, I started to put the box back in my purse, humiliation a copper taste in the back of my mouth.

"No," he said. "No, please, I'd like to open it now."

I handed it back to him and wiped my sweating hands on my gown. Which was shit for that kind of thing, actually. The netting stuck to my fingers.

Clayton pulled one end of the red ribbon that made the elaborate bow on top of the small box and it was like he was pulling my stomach with it. I reached into my purse and grabbed my glasses.

My own armor, maybe.

Or maybe I just wanted to see his face clearly when he opened my present.

He pulled off the thin lid and lifted the antique gold pocket watch out of the box.

"Veronica," he breathed.

"I saw it in a shop on Lucas Street. I mean, it's a little silly, I guess. But it does keep time. The guy at the store said it was owned by a cattle rancher in the area in the 1800's."

He turned the watch over and hit the small knob that popped open the front.

"That inscription was there," I said, wanting some distance from it if it was too much. Though the inscription was part of the reason I bought it. Because the woman who gave her husband this watch over a hundred years ago had had more courage than I did.

"For you, forever," he read.

"It's—"

He said nothing, just stepped toward me, stalked toward me, really, so fast and with such power I took a step back and my head hit one of the mirrors. And then he was kissing me. His hands cupped my face, like he was holding me still. Like I might possibly run?

Please.

These kisses, like he was trying to communicate something to me with his tongue, were a huge part of the reason I said yes when he asked me to marry him. Because this felt so important and real. His hands on my body. His tongue against mine.

It filled me with power, the kind of power that was bigger than I am.

It was epic.

He pulled back, rested his forehead against mine. "Thank you," he breathed. His breath smelled like mint and me.

"Thank you," I said back, and we smiled at each other. I beamed with all my heart, and his lip curled in a half grin, barely there.

"I might have messed up your hair," he said, pulling me away from the mirror. The flower he'd tried to put back fell to the floor.

"It's fine," I said. "Leave it. I don't think that flower was meant to be."

He clicked open the watch. "We need to head downstairs."

"Right." I smoothed my dress and reached to take off my glasses.

"Leave them," he said.

"Jennifer—"

"Hardly matters. Leave them. The whole point of tonight is for you to enjoy yourself. To have the kind of party that you deserve. I want you to enjoy tonight and you can't do that if you can't see." He touched my glasses, straightening them on my face.

"Well, when you put it that way." I twisted my lips. "Though I don't know how much of tonight will be enjoyable."

"Try," he said.

The idea of flaunting this relationship to Dallas's elite made me want to cringe. But I considered it my going-away gift to Dad and Jennifer. I'd do this dumb thing because they wanted it, and then I was done.

Because in one month's time my life as a King would be over and I'd be a Rorick.

Veronica Rorick.

With so many hard consonant sounds I was practically a fortress. I loved it.

He kissed me again. "See you down there."

After he walked out of the dressing room I folded forward, putting my hands on my knees.

Jesus. That man I was going to marry was so damn potent.

"Oh, my gosh! Ronnie!"

The whirling dervish that was my half sister rushed into

the room. She was just a few months younger than my sister, Bea, because my father was a cheating asshole and barely waited until my mother was in the ground before making his mistress the next Mrs. King so he could continue his search for a son in the wombs of his wives.

I should hate Sabrina, by rights, but it was impossible to hate Sabrina.

Shallow as a puddle, but sweet as sugar.

"You are a dream!" She was all lit up from the inside because the girl loved a party and tonight's was going to be a good one. A blowout, as she called it. "You're gorgeous. That dress! Your hair! That necklace! Are you sure about the glasses?"

"Sabrina," I sighed.

"Of course, your call. Totally your call." She stood in front of me and beamed. She was lovely and I couldn't help but smile back at her. We both had my father's dark hair, but her eyes were dark, too. Sabrina used to be a roly-poly preteen but in the last few years she had sculpted herself into the kind of perfection that made Jennifer giddy.

But perfection was so hard.

"I saw your gorgeous guy leaving. Is that why your lipstick is a mess?"

"Is it?" I pulled open my purse for the lipstick Sabrina had loaned me.

"Let me. You can't draw a lip to save your life."

Sabrina plucked the lip liner and gloss from the inside of my bag and got right up into my personal space. That was kinda Sabrina's thing. No boundaries.

"Sooooo..." she said.

"Yeah."

"I heard Dylan was invited."

Our half brother.

"He won't come."

Sabrina projected so much hope. She'd followed him around like a puppy the summer he'd stayed with us. We all had. He still left and never came back. "Hank said—" Sabrina had refused to call our father by any other name.

"He won't come because of Dad, Sabrina. Trust me. If there's one thing you can count on with Dylan, it's that he wants no part of being a King."

She pouted and I did, too. Which must have been the right thing to do because she beamed at me as she finished the makeup repair.

"You look perfect."

"You know..." I said, like it was a surprise—which it was "...I feel kinda perfect."

She wrapped me in her thin arms and I hugged her back. "Garrett Pine is here," she whispered.

Oh, boy.

In addition to Dallas society, we'd invited the entirety of the town of Dusty Creek, the arid clutch of churches and bars with one school, a medical clinic, and a grocery store that was about five miles away from the ranch.

Bea, Sabrina, and I all went to high school there with varying degrees of success and happiness.

And Garret Pine was a big part of that town.

And Sabrina loved him like a lunatic.

"He brought his fiancée."

"Oh, honey," I breathed. "I'm so sorry."

"I'm not," she said. "I'm happy for him. Delighted." She smiled so bright it almost blinded me to the heartache she couldn't quite hide.

"Don't do anything crazy," I told her.

"I won't."

"Sabrina," I sighed. "I mean it. No more stunts."

She pulled a face. "I won't do anything except make him sorry he'll never be mine by being charming and amazing."

"Well, you do look amazing."

"So, do you, Ronnie," she said. "Emma Stone's publicist is here, too. And some TV executives. I'm going to go show them my star power."

I hoped that didn't mean her underwear.

And then she was gone, leaving the smell of her perfume and a sense of glitter in the air behind her.

I trusted Sabrina's reaction to my reflection more than my own judgment, so I didn't bother looking back into the mirror. Outside the dressing-room door, I turned left instead of right and headed down the back staircase.

"Veronica!" called a voice behind me and I turned, wishing I'd moved just a little faster.

James Court.

Ugh.

"Hello, James," I said with a reserved smile. Which didn't seem to matter. I could be cold and reserved and downright rude, and it never seemed to matter to this guy.

James worked at King Industries and was one of my father's favorites.

"The boy's got swagger," Dad always said.

Which meant he had an ego and sense of entitlement a mile wide.

I hated him and I had no idea why, in the last six months, he'd gotten so interested in me.

"Congratulations," he said, tipping his glass of scotch toward me—a little too much and some of the scotch slipped out. "The best man won. I should have seen that coming, I suppose."

He was drunk.

I took a step back, keeping my smile small. "If you're referring to Clayton, you're right."

He took another step forward, so close I could smell his hot breath. His blue eyes narrowed. *Mean*, I thought. *This guy is just mean.*

"You're going to figure out sooner or later your old man made a mistake picking that fucker."

"Jimmy, you're drunk," I said and put my hand up to push him away. I took four quick backward steps before I turned.

"You're not even the hot sister," he yelled after me. Like that was a newsflash.

Around the edge of the hallway I stopped to get my breath and calm myself down. So many assholes were trying to ruin my night.

I needed my sister and a drink.

And some cheese.

The kitchen was full of black-vested and white-gloved staff, and I ducked out the back door, grabbing a skewer of grilled halloumi and figs as a server walked by.

Delicious.

Another thing they didn't tell you about orgasms. They made everything better.

Even cheese, which I honestly didn't think could *be* better.

The moon was swollen and low in the endless indigo sky and the air smelled like the grills behind the long screened-in porch—hickory smoke and twilight. The stables in the distance looked like a mansion, with turrets and bright, sparkling windows. All the horses, the stable cats, and Sally the collie lived pretty damn well here on The King's Land.

I pulled open the wide door and the cats came out to greet me. Sally, in the corner, lifted her head, thumped her tail once, and then sighed, tucking her nose under her leg. I heard the party in the far stall and rolled my eyes.

"Bea!" I shouted and there was a sudden silence from the back. The sound of guilt.

"Guys," my sister said. "Relax. She's not, like, my mom."

"I'm the closest thing you've got." I turned the corner and found my sister in her dark blue Versace gown with the hem pulled up around her knees, sitting on top of a bale of hay, the chalkboard from the office behind her.

A bottle of bourbon was tucked between her thighs.

Of course. Of-fucking-course.

The stall next door was full of a mare in the first stages of giving birth. Oscar, Tony, and a bunch of the other guys were milling between the two stalls.

My sister looked like me but scaled to a different size. She was small. Short and slight. Her eyes—and her attitude —were the biggest things about her.

Bea was eighty percent attitude, ten percent eyes, and the rest of her was fun.

The combination was catnip for a certain kind of man.

The dress she wore made her catnip to the rest of them.

"Bea." I propped my hand against the doorway. "What are you doing?"

"Well, Cosmic is having a baby." Bea pointed over the stall. "And I'm just taking a few bets."

This shouldn't be a surprise. Drinking bourbon during my engagement party and playing bookie was completely par for Bea's course.

"Has the party started?" she asked and took a swig of bourbon. The hay was stuck all over her dress and her super-expensive shoes with the red soles had been kicked into the corner.

"Yeah," I said.

"Oops." Bea winced and hopped off the hay bale. Once we were face-to-face she only came up to my shoulders, but she hugged me, smiling at me all the while.

"You look hot, sis," she said.

"Thanks, Bea." It was impossible to stay mad at her. My sister sparkled like midnight. Like the fun and possibility of a night, just as it was getting interesting.

She turned to Oscar and Tony. "No playing with the board. If that baby is a boy and born before midnight you owe me a shit ton of money."

The guys laughed and she handed Tony her bottle of bourbon so she could put on her shoes and stand another three inches taller.

"Let's go celebrate." She smelled like hay and horse, bourbon and perfume. Eau de Bea. "Pretty necklace," she said, smiling at me.

"You think?" I put my palm over it.

"*You* think, and that's all that matters." Bea pulled us to a stop just outside the back door. "You deserve this."

"A big awful party?"

"A big beautiful man. A big beautiful love."

My chest felt too small to hold my heart. "It's going to be all right, isn't it?"

My sister—dangerous, impetuous, and reckless, but also wise—cupped my face in her hands. "Better than all right," she said. "It's going to be perfect."

We walked back into the kitchen and down the hallway to the sounds of the party. We turned a corner and nearly ran into Jennifer.

"There you are." Jennifer's smile barely made a dent in her face. "Veronica, your father would like to see you in his study."

"How about me?" Bea asked, sarcastic and smiling. "What should I do?"

"Clean yourself up and try not to embarrass your father."

Bea wrinkled her nose. "Boring. I'll go with Ronnie."

We plucked the last two glasses of champagne from a waiter's tray and turned left down the hallway, away from the party, to my father's study. The door was on the other end of the hallway, and Bea and I were sipping our drinks and whispering about Jennifer's Botox addiction, but still we were able to hear Clayton's voice.

"That was the deal, Hank," he said.

He sounded mad and I picked up my pace. Clayton rarely got angry, but when he did, it took him a while to cool off and I didn't want him angry tonight. I wanted him smiling. His hand on the small of my back. His breath against my skin as he leaned down to whisper in my ear.

"I'm marrying your daughter. I'm securing your assets for another generation, if not more. We signed a contract!"

Bea and I shared one shocked look and then I pick up the pace, spilling champagne everywhere as I practically ran down the hallway.

"You are clearly trying to renegotiate the baby bonus." Dad's laugh was familiar. Satisfied. The laugh he laughed when he had all the power and didn't mind using it.

We got to the doorway of the study just as Clayton grabbed my father by the lapels of his tux.

"You wanted her married. I'm doing that. That was the deal. Now give me the deed to the goddamned land!" Clayton shouted.

The champagne glass fell from my suddenly numb fingers and found the small slice of wood between the carpeted hallway and the Oriental rug on the floor of father's study.

It shattered spectacularly.

I felt Bea behind me. Could sort of tell she was trying to hold me up. Or back. Hard to say.

The world was moving so fast. Too fast.

"What's happening?" I whispered.

If I'd had doubts about what was happening—if I'd thought I could find one shred of hope to cling to—that vanished when I saw Clayton's face.

The guilt was all over his cruel, handsome features. In the dark pools of his eyes. His rude-boy lips were a straight ugly line.

"What are you doing here?" he asked.

"What are *you* doing here?" Bea demanded, but Clayton didn't even blink.

"You should go back out to the party," he said to me. Like I was a child. Or a pet he could send away.

"Tell me what's happening. Tell me about...your deal," I said.

"Veronica." My father sat down behind his desk, looking far too pleased with himself. He twisted his pinky ring around his finger. "You can't be this naïve."

"What is he talking about?" Bea asked, grabbing my hand.

"He's marrying you for money," Dad said. "Specifically, my money. By way of my company. Oh, stop, Veronica. Don't look so damn hurt. I have to protect King Industries, and the best way I can do that is get someone I trust in the family. You have your charms, but you didn't think Clayton was suddenly interested in my plain, dull daughter. He didn't choose you—"

"Stop!" Clayton snapped. "Not another word."

My dad shut up, but the words were out.

Plain and *dull* didn't even hurt. The rest of it, though...

He didn't choose you.

"This is when you tell me it's not what it seems," I said to Clayton. Practically begging him to pull the wool back over my eyes. "Or...there's an explanation. That this isn't true."

Clayton was silent.

"Say something!" I yelled.

"It's true."

I put my hand against my stomach and looked down at the pretty confection of a dress, expecting blood. Rivers of it. Because surely he'd killed me.

"Veronica," Clayton said, and when I looked at him he'd pulled himself together and it was Clayton Rorick, impervious and distant, looking back at me.

Cold. So damn cold.

Had I dreamed he cared?

That he loved me?

Stupid, Veronica. You really are so stupid.

What made sense between a man like him and a woman like me? That he would feel something for my above-average wit and my below-average body?

Or that my father was paying him to marry me?

"The arrangement I have with your father has nothing to do with us," Clayton said.

I opened my mouth to laugh. I really thought I was going to laugh. Because I wanted to be that woman who could laugh at the man who'd just ripped out her heart, but it came out a sob.

I swallowed it. "What, exactly, is the arrangement between you and my father?"

"I don't think—"

"Tell me!" I shrieked, going full banshee on him.

"Upon our engagement and the securing of his property to the King bloodline, he will give me some property I have been trying to buy from him for a number of years."

"Securing?"

"A baby," my sister spat, and my heart shattered.

Clayton stepped forward like he might touch me, and I jerked back so hard I bashed into the doorjamb and sparks of pain filled my head. My knees buckled.

"Veronica!" He rushed toward me. "Are you all right?"

Thank God for Bea. My sister pulled me into her arms and put a hand out to stop Clayton.

"No!" she yelled. Unbelievably he listened and just stood there, a foot from me, strong and gorgeous and...evil. So damn evil.

Remember this. Remember this man didn't choose you.

"The engagement is over," I said.

"Now, Ronnie." My father stood up. "You walk away from this and you're walking away from King Industries. You'll never own this company."

"I don't give a shit about your company."

"But you do give a shit about that foundation."

For a second, I wavered. Because the foundation was my mother's legacy. My legacy.

Could I just...walk away from that? From all my plans? From the future I'd worked so hard for?

Bea put her arm around me. "Don't listen to him. Don't listen to any of them. Mom would want you to have more than this."

She was right. Of course she was right.

"Get me out of here, Bea," I whispered, feeling like I might pass out. Wishing that I could.

And my sister did. She put me in her car and drove me far, far away from The King's Land.

From my engagement party.

From my fiancé, who didn't even try and stop me.

From the life that was never meant for me.

I should have known better.

WANT MORE? Buy HERE!
http://geni.us/Fnh2P

SEX.
LIES.
BETRAYAL.
Welcome to The King family...

The
TYCOON
KING FAMILY, BOOK ONE

M. O'KEEFE
USA TODAY BESTSELLING AUTHOR

CPSIA information can be obtained
at www.ICGtesting.com
Printed in the USA
LVHW082338190519
618428LV00009B/128/P